LAST FLIGHT OF THE SNOWBIRDS

A NOVEL

ROBB FELDER

AUTHOR OF THE OTTER FALLS SERIES

Published by: Otter Falls Publishing
Cambridge, Minnesota 55008

This is a work of fiction; Names, characters, places and incidents in this book are products of the author's imagination, or used fictitiously, and any resemblance to actual persons living or dead, business establishments, events, or locales is purely coincidental.

ISBN 978-0-578-21284-5

Printed in the United States of America

To all of our beautiful children and grand and great grandchildren, both conceived and adopted.

To all Snowbirds everywhere who escape to the sun and warmth and dare to explore.

PROLOGUE

For thousands albeit tens of thousands of years, the natives of this northern forbidden land of ice and snow and bitter cold have chosen to pack up their belongings and trek southward. They go, seeking a warmer, more hospitable climate, away from the dark, cold days of winter. They migrate to a land of blue skies and eternal sunshine.

Some snowbird trekkers have a preplanned agenda and return year after year to the same retirement villages. Others book into rental properties on a per year basis.

These more adventurous birds create their own agendas and choose to explore the natural beauty of the southwest; the Colorado River valleys and the deserts and mountains at their own discretion. Trekkers Mike and Audrey are of this species of the Snowbirds.

Lying within the bowels of a deep dark canyon, there is a very dark secret. - - - -.

What these Snowbirds discover there, will take them on a very dark journey down the road to Perdition. But even with the devil himself in pursuit, they come full circle and come face to face with an opportunity for redemption.

NOVEMBER – IT BEGINS

Softly it whispers as it slowly sifts down from an ever-darkening cloud cover. Soon the barrel of his rifle is covered with the white stuff. Slowly the woods lapses into utter silence. Every sound has been muffled. Nothing is moving. The woodland critters all begin bedding down. It becomes pointless to sit there, in the tree stand covered with snow, with no possibility of seeing or hearing a deer. Mike brushes the snow off his rifle. Just as he was about to unload his rifle and call it quits, he sees a slight movement down and across the ravine that his tree stand is overlooking. There, through the now heavy snowfall and 'white-out', he can gradually see a form taking shape. The form appears to move with ease among the trees and brush. Then, as a gust of wind brings the shape closer into view, he can finally make out the features of the 'ghostly silent' figure. It now appears to be the figure of a deer, a very large deer. The ghostly looking, snow covered animal moves carefully and silently down into the ravine. Mike slowly and carefully brings up his rifle into the firing position. Even with the scope, he has to wait for the deer to emerge from the thick snow-covered brush along the side of the ravine. When the creature again appears in the scope, Mike is filled with dismay and disappointment.

"It has no antlers Mike says to himself, but almost out loud, It's a doe, a beautiful big doe, and I don't have a doe permit this year."

He brings the rifle back down into his lap, as he once again contemplates unloading it and calling it quits because of the poor visibility. But as the big doe silently makes its way down the trail across the ravine and up to the ridge just down about thirty yards from Mike's stand, he rethinks the whole scenario that may be unfolding in front of him.

"Where there is a doe coming down the trail this time of year, it's a sure bet there's a buck following her."

So, he waits, - - ten, - - twenty minutes. This time he was not disappointed. Sure enough, there on the opposite edge of the ravine where the doe had appeared earlier, Mike saw movement again. The ghostly snow-covered shape moved even closer and stopped on the other side of the ravine and turned sideways and presented the perfect shot as Mike slowly and carefully raised the rifle scope to his eye. He is not disappointed this time.

"Yes, yes," he says as he counts about twelve points on the big bucks rack, "big boy, you're all mine".

But, instead of following down the trail into the ravine, where the doe had gone, the big buck moved along the top edge of the ravine, further down and stopped and turned as if studying the situation.

"He must have caught my scent," Mike thought, as he aligns the crosshairs of the scope on the chest of his trophy, "I'd better take my shot now."

But just as he pulls the trigger, a gust of wind swirled the snow into his face and carried the ghostly figure down into the ravine and out of sight into the whiteout. Mike removes the clip from his rifle and ejects the spent round from the chamber. He carefully lowers the rifle down from the tree stand with the cord attached there for that purpose then climbs down himself. He slings the rifle over his shoulder and makes his way down the trail to the next hunter in line on the ridge.

"Looks like this first day of the hunt is over." Mike declared to his son, Chris, not mentioning his missed shot at the ghostly visitor. He knew from experience that it would only make himself look like a fool.

"Yah, ya can't see your hand in front of your face anymore. I'll come down and head up the ridge and round up Roger and the rest of the guys. You go on ahead, we'll meet you back at deer camp."

* * * * * *

Meanwhile, across the state, Mike's wife Audrey and daughter Linda, along with sister-in-law Mary, are just getting settled into another camp. This one is called a quilt camp, or retreat. Camp Lebanon is a Baptist retreat camp. The three gals have just gotten their sewing machines unpacked, and along with about one hundred other ladies will begin a weekend of sewing and socializing and quilt making. They are not too concerned about the snow coming down heavily outside. They will be inside, cozy and warm for the weekend.

* * * * * *

Mike turned and started down the trail to where their trucks were parked. He waited there for the rest of the hunters. They all drove in convoy fashion back to their deer shack and stoked up their fire to wait out the snowstorm.

Cards were brought out, along with beverages, and poker games commenced. The snow continued to fall for the rest of the day and on into the night. By morning, the snow had piled up almost two feet deep and the wind was howling and churning the snow into a complete white-out. The hunters could hardly find the outhouse. They had to dig the firewood for the day out from under a four foot deep snowdrift. This would be another no-hunting day, another day of poker, beer and camp-food. A huge pot of chili was cooked for noon lunch and lasted through supper. By the next morning the blizzard abated and the camp-weary hunters returned to their stands. Under crystal-clear skies, the prey was easily spotted in the new snow. Soon, shots could be heard. Dead animals were gutted and dragged back to the trucks. Mike's had eight points on his rack.

"This is good," he thinks, "Not the twelve pointer I should have had two days ago, but, Audrey and I should have plenty of venison jerky to take to Arizona this winter."

With all the tags now filled, they all load up their trucks for the trip back home. Mike cleans up and locks up the deer shack for another year. On the slow trip home on the snowy, icy roads, he again reviews all the things that need to be organized for the annual trek to Arizona for the winter. Upon arriving home at their lake home on Thunder Lake, he checks his deer in at a deer processing center and orders a variety of cuts of venison, but mostly venison jerky which will be the easiest to pack for the Arizona trip. The venison, they tell him, should be processed in time for the trip, right after Thanksgiving.

Audrey arrives home a short time later after dropping Linda off. After unpacking, she and Mike settle down with cups of coffee and discuss their weekend, and begin discussing and planning the trip to Arizona.

“There’s a lot to get done in just three weeks,” Audrey says, “If we want to leave right after Thanksgiving.”

Mike calls the rental agency in Lake Havasu City to make sure they still have the condo reserved. He then logs on to his bank and transfers the money for the first month’s rent along with the damage deposit to seal the deal. Meantime Audrey begins working on a list of must-haves to pack. There isn’t a lot of room in their Honda CRV. Their cat, Maggie will require the entire back seat. So, it’s mostly clothes and a few craft and hobby things to keep them busy for the four months in Lake Havasu City. Fortunately, in Havasu, there are plenty of outdoor activities to keep them busy. As in the past, they will be spending most of their time outdoors, walking the river walk through Rotary Park, along the lakeshore of Lake Havasu and under the London Bridge. There are also the hundreds of square miles of the Colorado River Valley with its beautiful rock formations and the deserts and mountains to be explored.

* * * * * * * *

November days rapidly slip away under grey skies and ever sliding temperatures. As Thanksgiving approaches, packing continues in earnest. The day of "the feast of the beast" most of the family gathers at Jeff and Darcy's house where Christmas gifts are handed out and received. Some opened now and some saved for actual Christmas. Good-byes are said by everyone.

"You guys drive safely," is Jeff's wish for his parents.

"We'll see you when we come down in February," promised Richard and Joan.

Betsey and John proclaim, "We'll see you in Havasu for spring break again."

Black Friday, as everyone heads for the malls the snow is again falling, giving Mike and Audrey an appropriate send-off. They head south on I-35 into Iowa trying to get ahead of the storm by Kansas City.

Mike, the procrastinator says, “Maybe we should wait until after the snowstorm has passed.”

Audrey says, “No, we want to get into our condo in Lake Havasu by December first.”

“Yah, well, you remember the last time we tried to beat out a storm,” Mike argues, “that was the year that we met up with a snowstorm in Amarillo that was supposedly coming down the eastern front of the Rockies from Albuquerque. We thought we could bypass the storm by heading south from Amarillo across Texas. The storm was predicted to head east from Amarillo into Oklahoma. We raced all the way south across Texas to El Paso on the Mexico border. We stopped there overnight. In the morning, we woke up to find that the snowstorm had followed us south. El Paso had received about ten inches of snow by morning. We had to wait another day there, because I-10 was closed. The snowstorm headed south from Amarillo instead of heading East. So much for ‘storm-dodging’.

“It seems like everyone has their favorite snow-storm to reminisce about,” Audrey says.

So - - -, in the end, Audrey wins out, of course, and the two snowbirds head south down I-35.

* * * * * *

And, so the great escape begins. The two snowbirds are escaping from Minnesota, the land of;

polar plunges, polar temperatures, polar vortexes, frost-bite, below-zero, wind-chill-factor, weather watching, cold fronts, frozen toes-cheeks-fingers, hypothermia, wind-chill warning, blizzard warning, howling blizzards, snow storms, Alberta clippers, white-outs, visibility, inches, light snow, heavy snow, crunchy snow, wet snow, window-defoggers, bone-chilling, jumper cables, snow plows, dead batteries, jump starts, black ice, spin-outs, fender-bender, stuck, road closures, school closures, winter coats - sweaters - hats - mittens and boots, long-johns, scraping ice and snow off of windshields, cross-country skiing, snow shoes, snowmobiling, ice fishing, ice-houses, ice-out, icicles, thin ice , ice-dams, snow emergency routes, ice covered roads, snow-packed roads, salted roads, pot-holes, salt haze on windshields, long lines at car washes every week, shoveling mountains of snow off of driveways and sidewalks, crunchy snow, wet snow, snow balls, snow men, snow shovel, snow blower, snow plow.

And at long last, - - -

The Spring Thaw.

They are leaving behind all the above joys of living in Minnesota, the 'State Of Hockey' and all of its associated terminologies. Seems like one cannot speak to anyone without including one or more of the above terms in their conversations, - - -.

(Ya, fer sure, you bet'cha', the language of Minnesota). So, have some 'hot-dish' and put on your long johns, parkas, choppers, bibs, sorel boots, and ski-masks and enjoy the weather. In Minnesota, it's always about the weather.

By the time they get to Des Moines, the snow subsides and they have clear sailing all the way through to Kansas City.

The next day, they head down the Kansas Turnpike to Oklahoma City. In the morning they pick up I-40 which will take them all the way west to the California border. Here, the Colorado River divides Arizona and California. But first, another overnight in Tucumcari, New Mexico, and another in Albuquerque.

After the last night on the road in Flagstaff, Arizona, the snowbirds wake up to about sixteen inches of snow. Flagstaff is not a very large city, with a population of about 70,320. However, it is the highest elevation city in the U.S. at about 7,000 ft. above sea level. Denver gets all the press for being the "mile high city", but Flagstaff is almost a mile and a half high. Flagstaff gets up to 100 inches of snow each winter, making it one of the snowiest cities in the contiguous 48 states. The twin cities of Minnesota, by comparison, get a meager sixty inches. I-40 is closed, so another day is spent cooped up in the motel room. Mike makes a call to their condo place to reassure them that they are on the way and will be late getting in. The snowbirds head west again in the morning, down the mountain.

As they are leaving Flagstaff, Audrey says, "I sure do hope that's the last snow we see until next November."

"Yah, I know, I'm sick to death of the never-ending snow we have to put up with. Maybe we should decide once and for all to just move to Lake Havasu."

"You know, we've had that conversation many times over the years. You know it'll never happen. We decided long ago that we would miss our kids and grandkids too much. We're just too old now to consider uprooting and moving. We'll just continue trekking back and forth for the rest of our days."

Just south of Kingman, Arizona, the two snowbirds exit I-40 and head south, down U.S. Highway 95, down the mountain into Lake Havasu City on the Colorado River. It is late afternoon as they descend into the river valley.

The sun is setting and creates a red-orange streak of clouds over Lake Havasu as it sets behind the Buckskin Mountains of California on the western side of the lake. Lake Havasu was formed when a dam built across the Colorado River at the town of Parker, Arizona, caused a large lake to form behind the dam upstream for about twenty five miles, similar to Lake Mead, which was formed behind the Hoover dam, upstream from Havasu. The city was named for the Havasupi Indian tribe who occupied the land surrounding the Colorado River before the white settlers came..

"Gosh, the sunsets are always so beautiful over the lake," Audrey comments.

"I know, it makes me feel warmer already, and they only get snow in Havasu City about once every twenty years."

Just after sunset, Mike and Audrey check in at the condo office and pick up their keys. Theirs is a second floor unit above the garage with a balcony with a lake view.

"This is so great," Audrey says, "We're so close to the Rotary Park on the lake, we can walk to the park."

After several trips up and down the stairs to unload their car and bring up Maggie their cat and her equipment, they decide it's too late to get groceries, so they opt for take-out. After unpacking, they make the necessary phone calls to let everyone know they have arrived. After some TV watching, they crash into bed.

"It feels so great to be in off the road after six days of driving," Mike comments.

"I know, the trip seems to get longer every year. I remember when we used to make it in four days."

"Yah, we were younger then. I can't believe we've been coming here off and on for twelve years already."

THE BRIDGE

Our two snowbirds sleep in very late the next morning.

"You'd think we were back in Minnesota and going into hibernation," Mike commented.

"Yah, but we better get going," Audrey states, "There's no hibernating here in sunny Arizona. We've got more to do to get set up. We've got to get some groceries, right after we go out and get some breakfast."

"And our good friends Bill and Mia Wilson want to join us for lunch," Mike adds.

After breakfast, they head for Food City and stock up on groceries for the first month.

After the food is put away, Audrey says, "Lets head down to Rotary Park and do a channel walk.

It's about a mile walk from the south end of the Park along the lake channel to the London Bridge. Lake Havasu City is all about the London Bridge. The city was founded by James McCulloch in 1956. He bought a very large tract of land on the eastern shore of Lake Havasu from the state of Arizona. McCulloch owned a very successful small-engine and equipment company in Los Angeles and wanted to move the manufacturing facility out of LA for tax reasons. Shortly after moving his company to Lake Havasu City, McCulloch heard about a bridge that was being torn down over in England and was being sold. He submitted a bid to purchase the old London Bridge. His thinking was that the bridge would make a great tourist attraction for his newly founded city. The London Bridge was loaded aboard a ship, block-by-block; each block carefully numbered, then shipped to Los Angeles, then on to Havasu.

Part of Lake Havasu City resided on a large peninsula that jutted out into the lake. The newly acquired bridge was reassembled on dry land and positioned where the peninsula met the shore line of the lake. After assembly, a channel was dug through the peninsula along the shoreline and under the newly rebuilt, old London Bridge and part of the Colorado River now flowed under the bridge. Another result of this project is that what was once a peninsula jutting out into Lake Havasu is now a large island in the lake.

Part of the water of Lake Havasu is pumped up and out of the valley and feeds into a canal that flows about eighty miles to Phoenix. Another part of the water is pumped out on the west side of the lake in California and makes its way across the Mohave Desert to Los Angeles. The balance of the lake water flows south all the way into Mexico and the Gulf of California.

* * * * * * *

Mike and Audrey meet up with their long-time friends in Lake Havasu, Bill and Mia. Mia had worked with Audrey for many years at Midway Hospital in St Paul and when that hospital closed, they both worked together at the 'same-day' surgery unit adjacent to St. Johns Hospital in the suburb of Maplewood. When Bill and Mia retired, they moved to Lake Havasu full-time. However, Mike and Audrey moved to their lake cabin in northern Minnesota when they retired.

The two couples meet at a brew-pub called Mudsharks.

"Well, we're glad you made it out to sunny Arizona again," Mia said.

"Yeah, and we're glad to see you two snowbirds didn't get snow-bound in El Paso this year," Bill chuckled.

"Well, not this year," Mike responded. "No more storm-dodging for us. Although, this year we spent an extra day, up in Flagstaff, waiting for them to plow out I-40."

"Yeah, that city is always a risk for a good snowstorm. That's all it does is snow in Flagstaff."

"Alright, already," Audrey quipped, "Enough with the snow-talk. I just want to talk about Arizona sunshine."

"Okay," Bill said, "How's this. The Striper Bass have really been 'on the bite' lately, down near Copper Canyon. I'm pretty booked up this week taking fishermen out, but how about early next week, you and I, Mike; take a run down there, and see what we can do. Then, maybe the following week, the four of us head down to a spot I know of near the Parker Dam. The Stripers hit pretty good there about mid-December. But, the rest of December is pretty well booked through the holidays."

Bill is a really avid fisherman. He fished almost every day when he and Mia first retired to Havasu. Now he has his own fishing guide service on the lake.

"What did you guys bring with this year for hobbies?" Bill asks.

"Well," Mike replies, "I brought my beer-making equipment again. So I'll be brewing up a batch of home brew as soon as we get settled

"How about while the guys are out to Copper Canyon next week," Mia said to Audrey, "You and I check out that new quilting and sewing shop up on McCulloch Blvd. I've got a new quilt that I've been working on, and I need some finishing pieces."

"Oh, that would be fun," Audrey replied, "I've brought my sewing machine again, along with some quilt squares, but I can always use some more fabric."

"So, do you guys have any plans yet, for the holidays?" Mike asked.

"Well, our kids and grandkids will probably be coming out from Wisconsin. How about you guys?"

"We pretty much had our Christmas with everyone before we left," Audrey said. We probably won't see anyone until Spring Break. How about New Year's? I heard they're having a big New Year's Eve party at our condo building. Why don't you guys come?"

"That'd be fun," Mia said, "Meantime, why don't we get together Saturday nights for cards like we've done in the past? We can invite our friends, Rick and Rhonda, like last year. Then we can rotate places every week like before."

"Okay," Mike said, "Looks like we've got everything planned out through the holidays.

We'll see you guys Saturday night, then. You guys have a great week"

With lunch over, they all split up. Audrey said, "I want to stop at the used book store on the way back to the condo."

"Good idea," Mike said, "We didn't pack any with this year. Then, after that, let's go over to Hobby Lobby. I want to see if they have any interesting paint-by-numbers I can work on. I've got to have something to do besides reading and putting together jigsaw puzzles all winter."

THE CRACK, AND OATMAN

By mid-December, our snowbirds have become restless. "We need to get out and do more hiking now while the weather is cooler," Audrey says, "There are so many good places to hike around Lake Havasu."

"I totally agree," Mike says, "How about we start with a hike through the "Crack". That's one of our favorites. We should leave early in the morning."

So, they got out their hiking boots and packed a lunch for a day-hike down through 'The Crack'. The Crack is a geological feature just south of Lake Havasu City, between highway 95 and the lake. There is a low ridge of ancient volcanic formation. This was formed as the volcanic lava bubbled up from an ancient volcano and formed a long ridge of the volcanic rock along the ancient Colorado River bed. As the hot lava cooled rapidly, it cracked as it shrunk and split the low ridge in two. The crevice that resulted is about a hundred yards long, though quite narrow, in places barely wide enough to squeeze through and about a hundred feet deep to the crest of the ridge. There is a 'wash' that begins farther to the east of highway 95, up the western slope of Crossman Mountain and passes under highway 95 and through the Crack and down into Lake Havasu. Most all of these washes in and around Lake Havasu are 'dry washes', they will only possibly have water in them when it rains quite heavily. In the heavy rains of the summer monsoons, this wash is one of many that carry rain water down the slope of Crossman Peak and into Lake Havasu. Over the eons of time, the washing of gravel through the crevice, or 'crack', as it's called, has polished the walls of the 'crack smooth. This wash, about a two mile hike from highway ninety five, takes you through the 'crack' to Lake Havasu south of town is a favorite trail for hikers.

The two hikers arrive at the wash that will take them down through the crack. This area just south of town is a large city park and recreational area. It contains a large race track for horses, autos and rodeos, as well as concerts. The park also includes a BMX track and numerous ball fields.

Mike and Audrey don their hiking gear; desert hats, backpacks and walking sticks. They have also packed a camera, binoculars and, of course, several bottles of water, because even though the temperature is cooler this time of year, this is still the desert and it is very dry all year around. After donning all their gear they leave the parking lot and approach the entrance to the hiking trails.

Mike questions, "Well, Audrey, which trail should we take this time?"

The wash that goes down through the crack has numerous channels that are all intertwined with each other in a large flatter area before dumping down into the crack. Because it's easy to get turned around and get lost in the numerous intertwining maze of channels, the developers of the park had the foresight to mark the trails with color-coded trail signs. Some of the trails go down into the wash all the way to the crack. Some others go up and stay on the higher perimeter of the wash. Still others meander up and down, in and out of the main wash and its tributaries. This gives hikers a variety of different terrains to choose from. While the bottoms of the channels are covered with loose sand and gravel, this can become tiresome to walk on, even though the sRichard bottoms are relatively flat.

"Why don't we try the green trail this time. I think we've tried all the others already."

"Okay, green it is. This is the same trail that we return from the lake on. It goes up the ridge and around the crack, and it travels the high-ground around the rim of the wash and offers a commanding view of the wash. The trail comes down and crosses the main wash just outside the entrance to the crack, so we can get off the trail and go down into the crack from this green trail. Don't forget the "slide" is almost impossible to climb back up on the return trip."

About half way through the crack there is a very sharp drop of about eight or ten feet down a solid rock drop in the trail. This rock formation has been polished smooth by eons of water mixed with the sand flowing down this drop. Going down is easy, you just slide down. But coming back up is just about impossible on the slippery polished rock of the slide. So most all hikers opt to take the Green trail on the return trip, to go up and over the crack.

From the green trail high above the wash they observe a lot of the wildlife. They see a coyote chasing a rabbit down in the wash. They see numerous road-runners scurrying about looking for an early morning snack. While the high perimeter of the washes are mostly barren rock and rubble, down in the washes there is quite a bit of foliage. The edges of the bottom of the washes are lined with Mesquite and Palo Verde trees and numerous creosote bushes. As well as some different types of desert grasses. And let's not forget about the multitude of different species of cactus plants scattered everywhere. As our two hikers approach the ridge that contains the crack, they stop for a short water break.

Mike says, "Let's take out our binoculars and scout some of the high craggy peaks of rock and see if we can spot a mountain goat or a mountain lion, or maybe a coyote."

"Oh, look," Audrey says, "Look up there, on our left, at that large rock formation that juts out near the top. I can see a large mountain goat and two smaller ones."

"Wow," Mike says, "That's pretty cool. I don't think we've ever seen the mountain goats on any of our previous trips. Good thing we got out here in the early morning when the wildlife is still active. Later in the day, they all get into shady spots to get out of the torrid afternoon sun. Most of them will sleep all day and get up at sundown to forage during the cooler night-time hours."

"Yeah, and I'm really glad we remembered our binoculars this time. We should be able to see a lot more wildlife down along the lakeshore when we get there."

After the water break, the trail takes them down into the wash near the mouth of the crevice. They enter the crack and after about twenty or thirty yards in and some sharp twists and turns they come to the ‘slide’. Sheer rock walls extend upward for about a hundred feet on both sides of them. Mike takes off his backpack and opens it and takes out a hank of large rope, about twenty feet long, that has been knotted about every two feet.

“I didn’t think that we should, at our age, attempt to slide down the slide. Our old bones are just too brittle and we are too stiff to navigate the very steep and irregular and slippery surface of the slide.”

He ties one end to a rock that is half imbedded in the floor of the crack, and tosses the other end down the slippery slide. They take turns climbing down the knotted rope. When they are both at the bottom of the slide, Mike takes hold of the rope and flips it up and off of the rock at the top of the slide and coils it back up and returns it to his backpack. After several twists and turns of the trail, the crack narrows as it keeps descending towards the lake. One section of the crevice is so narrow that they need to turn sidewise to squeeze through it. Another section has walls that go up at an angle that overhangs the trail and they have to squeeze through by leaning on the opposite wall. Some sections of the trail have pools of standing water. Luckily, it is barely knee-deep.

Finally they emerge at the end of the crack. The trail broadens out into a wide flat, section of the wash. The wash turns a corner and descends down to the lakeshore. Here, there is an abundance of foliage, mostly willow trees. There is a picnic area with tables and canopies at the lakeshore and the couple takes a table and relax after the arduous hike through the crack. The return trip will be a much easier hike.

"Okay, let's eat," Mike says, as he unpacks his backpack and pulls out his lunch.

'You go ahead, Mike, I'm going to have a look around first. I can't believe all the wildlife down here compared to up in the desert, especially all the birds."

"I know, there must be hundreds of birds flying around. Look at the seagulls, osprey, and ducks. I recognize two or three types of ducks from back in Minnesota; mallards, cormorants, and the coot. Well, let's eat, Audrey, then we can explore along the shore and watch the birds. I think a lot of these ducks are migrating birds from up north, wintering here in the warm Colorado River Valley."

"Well, I guess you could say, then, that they are just like us, but these are truly 'snowbirds'."

They finish their lunch and then take a walk out onto a short rocky peninsula that juts out into the small bay. They each have their binoculars in hand. At the end of the peninsula they wave to fishing boats returning up the lake from the Copper Canyon area with their catches of the Striper Bass that the lake is so famous for. They watch the seagulls and ducks feeding on clams and diving for crayfish.

Suddenly, Audrey says, “Oh look, Mike, up there in that tall mesquite tree about half way up the hillside. isn’t that an eagle?”

They both train their binoculars on the tree top. “Sure enough,” Mike says, “That’s a Bald Eagle.”

Just as they spot the Bald Eagle, it leaps off its perch and goes streaming down into the bay just about a hundred yards from the peninsula where they are standing and snatches a fish in its powerful talons from just below the surface.

“Wow,” Audrey says, “What a sight. I think I got a pretty good picture of it on my cell camera with video on.”

“Oh, that’s super. It seems like all of God’s creatures are having breakfast right now. I’m so glad we got out here early, during their feeding time of the day.”

They continue their walk around the small bay and then decide to head back, catching the trail again, just behind the picnic area and follow it up through the willow-grove to the wash. Here they follow the wash back toward the crack. Just before the crack they spot the trail sign for the green trail again and follow it up out of the wash and begin the climb up the steep trail, up to the top of the ridge. It's a long steep climb and they take several rest stops along the way. Thankfully, there are numerous large boulders alongside the trail to sit on and drink their water. There are these boulders strewn everywhere on the ridge.

"I think these rocks and boulders were scattered here," Mike exclaims, "Back when one of these ancient volcanos exploded, probably the same one that had created this ridge, back in the Mesozoic period, or earlier. But, then, of course, it cracked and created the giant crevice."

"Yes, it cracked," Audrey continued, "And that's why we are here, - - - -all because it cracked."

* * * * * *

"We should go to Oatman," Audrey said, about two weeks before Christmas. "I would like to look for some unique gift items for some of the kids and grandkids, and Oatman has a lot of unique little shops."

"Okay, you're right, and you know I love going there to look at all their Navajo pottery, and I do love eating at the old Oatman Hotel restaurant. They have the best buffalo burgers anywhere, and I also love those huge potato chips they call 'donkey ears' but we need to hurry and get the gifts in the mail in order for them to arrive by Christmas."

Oatman, Arizona is a 'ghost town'. It is one of several listed around Arizona. Some are truly "ghost towns", totally abandoned and deserted. Oatman, located on old "route 66", about fifty miles north of Lake Havasu City, however, is not truly a "ghost town", in that sense, because it is not really abandoned. Although, it is really a 'wild-west' town of yesteryear, well preserved as the way it must have been in the eighteen hundreds. The townsfolk stage a mock bank robbery every day at noon, and a gunfight in the street, as they capture the 'bad guys'. Most all of the general stores and some of the saloons have been converted into "tourist" shops, selling souvenir items. Most of the old saloons are now restaurants.

The most famous landmark building is the old Oatman Hotel. History has it, that Clark Gable and Carol Lombard, Hollywood actor and actress from the 1920's and 30's, spent their honeymoon at the Hotel. The room has been preserved just as it was back in the 1930's. Many of those early western movies were shot in this part of Arizona. Another unique feature of the old hotel is the restaurant. The walls, ceiling, doorways posts and the bar area are covered with dollar bills, literally thousands and thousands of the dollar bills. Guests will take a dollar bill and write their name and address and date on them and staple them to wherever they can find an empty space. Guests have been doing this ever since the nineteen fifties.

Wild burros come down from the mountains and roam up and down the streets. They are not really wild, however. They come looking for food, and you can purchase a bag of carrots in the shops and hand-feed and pet them.

With that shopping completed, and the gifts in the mail, Mike and Audrey are all set for the holidays

A LA JUNTA CHRISTMAS

High up in the Sierra Madre of Mexico, in the small mountain pass village, of La Junta, just west of Chihuahua, about four hundred miles south of El Paso, another family is also preparing for Christmas. The Mendoza family is busy preparing to make a Christmas Eve delivery.

"Xavier, if you have the plane ready," Maria says, "I will call to have the product ready for pickup." She has on jeans and a bright red sweater.

"Si," he replies, "I was out to the air strip early this morning and gassed up the plane. Everything is ready for the trip." He is wearing jeans and a bright red plaid shirt to complement her sweater. "I think it was very smart of them to set up this delivery for Christmas Eve. Everyone along the border will be busy with their Christmas celebrations and parties."

"I hope this will be our last trip. With the money from this last delivery, we will finally have enough money to move our family to the U.S. In the last letter from my sister Juanita in Las Vegas, she said she has found a place for us to live."

"Si, and I, too have received a letter. A letter from the air service company in Las Vegas saying they have an opening for an aircraft mechanic. I know I won't be able to get my flying license to fly any planes in the U.S. until I become a U.S. citizen, but I can work as a mechanic until then."

With that said, the Mendoza couple gather their children; Juanita, age 13, Juan, age 11, Madeline, age 8 and Antonio, age 6 to say good-by.

Maria tells them, "We'll be back late in the day, hopefully in time for Midnight Mass. You are to stay in the house today. Juanita, you are in charge. You will need to prepare the meals while we are gone, and Juan, you will help with the cleanup. You can all work on making Christmas decorations and finish decorating the tree. Juanita and Juan, you can read the Christmas stories to Madeline and Antonio. Say your prayers at bed-time. And all of you practice your English. We will soon be living in the USA."

Xavier and Maria then get in their 1980's Chevy truck for the trip into Chihuahua to pick up the goods that they will be delivering into the U.S.

On the way there, Xavier says to Maria, "Remember back before we were delivering their "product", by plane. They would have to send out the "Mules" to cross the border on foot and make the deliveries to the drop-sites."

"I know," Maria says, "I like this way so much better. The U.S. president, Senior Trump, has done us a very big favor. He is putting up his famous wall. So now the "product" has to be delivered by plane. This means that delivery plane companies like ours, all over Mexico are making a lot of money delivering the 'product', over the Donald Trump wall."

They drive to the Chihuahua suburban town of Pedro Meoqui. There they pull up to an old rusty, unmarked, unpainted steel building. Someone meets them at the door. They have to wait several hours. They are not introduced. Names are not used during these interchanges. Xavier and Maria do not know where the product comes from, nor do they know which drug cartel they are working for. They have never met their suppliers and just assume that it is from somewhere in Columbia. They just deliver the product to the U.S. at the pre-arranged drop site, and return with the "package", which they assume contains the money, in U.S. dollars from the sale of the "Product".

Xavier and Maria are directed to back their truck up to an overhead door where another person helps them load the fifty bundles of the product into their truck. Each bundle weighs ten kilograms, or about twenty two pounds, for a total load of about a thousand pounds.

"This may be too much weight for our small plane," Maria complains.

"What the hell do you want?" the worker replies, "This is what they give us, so this is what you get. Do you want this damn load, or not? I can tell my boss, and he can come out and tell you that this is your last load, or, maybe he will just come out and shoot you. Look, you better just take the damn load and go with it. You're being paid extra for this extra big load for the holidays."

With that said, he hands them an envelope and says, "Now get the hell out of here before someone hears us arguing."

"Alright, alright," Xavier says to both Maria and the dock worker, "Come on, Maria, let's get out of here. We can just drop about fifty kilograms of fuel for the flight. On the way back, maybe we can stop in Nogales, or Hermosillo and re-fuel."

Xavier and Maria get back in the truck and head to their landing strip. The old Chevy truck struggles through the steep winding mountain roads with its extra heavy load, to the landing strip near the village of Cuauhtemoc. The sun is just now beginning to set over the mountain peaks to the West when they pull up to their plane. Maria begins loading the 'product' into the plane from the truck, while Xavier finds several empty fuel cans and begins draining off the required fifty kilos of the fuel and carries them over to the side of the runway. He then gets in and starts up the two-engine Cessna and says to Maria, "I want the engines really warm for this trip. It'll be a struggle to get up in the air and over the mountains, and "the wall" with the extra weight. I'll be back there in a few minutes to give you a hand loading."

After the loading is complete and the bundles of the product securely strapped in, Xavier pulls the truck off to the side of the runway. The runway is just a dirt strip, somewhat level, on a high plateau of the Sierra Madre. He returns to their plane and checks the wind sock at the side of the runway. The wind is out of the northwest, so Xavier points the Cessna into the wind at the south end of the runway. He revs the engines and releases the brakes. The plane leaps forward into the slight wind and they do a rapid climb to about ten thousand, then twenty thousand feet. This will get them safely over the peaks of the Sierra Madre. Xavier and Maria put on their oxygen masks because their plane is not pressurized with oxygen. The Cessna works hard to make the steep assent with their heavy load. The sun is setting over the Sierra Madre mountains as they reach their cruising altitude.

They will maintain this altitude as they head northwest between the town of Hermosilla and Nogales to avoid detection by the radar of those two airports. They do not file a flight plan of course, so no one is aware of their presence in the sky. Their plane is equipped with its own radar and GPS for navigation. After passing an imaginary line between those two towns, they turn and head north by northwest to where there is a wide expanse of about two hundred fifty kilometers along the U.S. and Mexico border between the towns of Nogales and San Luis. Here there will probably be no radar detection along this stretch of the border. Xavier climbs the plane to about thirty thousand feet over the border, to be out of range of any radar from the "Trump" border wall below them. They cannot see the border wall because it is now totally dark out and they are now well above the clouds.

Once safely across the border, they head toward a spot about halfway between the Arizona town of Gila Bend and Yuma. They know that there is no airport along this stretch of I-10, and therefore no radar. Their GPS will guide them.

"Look Xavier," Maria says pointing to the radar screen, "It looks like we are running into a very large thunder storm."

"Well, we can stay above it until we get to our destination, but then we will have to plunge down through it to land."

Soon, they can see the lights of the small towns all along I-8 as they pass over it on their way north. After about a half hour they cross the I-10 well east of Quartzite and in a few minutes, pass over the town of Wenden, on U.S. Highway 60, which has no airfield and therefore no radar. They head due north into the Buckskin Mountains area. Below them is Cunningham Pass at twenty five hundred sixty feet. Also, below them they can see the flashes of lightning from the huge thunder storm coming up out of Blythe, California and across from the town of Parker, Arizona.

Maria tunes in the signal from the transponder that they had set up on their secret runway, high above the Bill Williams River, on a somewhat level plateau hidden in the brush just at the bottom end of their runway. The transponder was set up with a solar panel and battery pack to transmit a constant signal which will allow them to hone in on their runway, even at night, and hopefully, even in the thunderstorm. As soon as Maria picks up the signal, Xavier begins descending the plane, down through the thunder storm clouds guided by the signal. The plane pitches and rolls from the turbulence, but stays on track and alignment to the runway. Just as they are about to set the plane down, a strong gust of side-wind turns the plane at a sharp angle to the runway. Xavier, however, manages to set their plane down on the runway okay, but as they are taxiing to the end of the runway in the pouring rain, the plane skids in the rain-soaked mud and the side-wind pushes them off the runway and into a shallow muddy wash where they come to a stop in the mud, tilted at an angle.

Xavier and Maria don their rain ponchos and get out with flashlights to assess the damages.

"Well, the plane seems to be structurally okay," he says, "The one wheel is pretty deep in the mud. I don't know if the power of the engines will pull us out. We are very low on fuel now and can't afford to burn up too much trying to pull out of the mud. The one other issue we have is that we are dangerously close to the edge of the cliff that drops into a canyon which feeds into the Bill Williams River. A really strong gust of wind could push the plane over the edge."

"Well, let's get our product unloaded and ready for the first exchange. I'll get the canopy set up, out away from the plane like on previous exchanges, and you can begin unloading. Because of the big load this time, there will be two exchanges, the first one is for thirty bundles of the product and the pickup is scheduled in about an hour, at seven o'clock."

Maria gets the canopy set up and securely tied down in the gusty wind. She also gets a folding table set up so the pickup person can examine the product before paying for it. She also gets out an electric lantern and hangs it under the canopy, but does not yet turn it on. They use only very limited lighting to move about and prepare the setup. You can tell they have done this before. They know just what to do to get set up. Xavier unloads thirty of the bundles and stacks them on the table under the canopy. They get their weapons out of the plane and get them loaded and ready. Xavier will accompany the pick-up person under the canopy. He is packing a Sig 45 in a shoulder holster and a smaller S & W 38 in a leg holster. Maria will stay in the plane and keep him covered with her AK assault rifle trained on the pick-up person, or persons. The assault rifle is equipped with a night scope.

Then, they wait. - - - - -

In about forty-five minutes, right on time, they see the headlights ambling along the very rugged road that comes from the town of Parker, off of Arizona highway 95 and follows the Bill Williams River valley up to the dam at Alamo Lake. Xavier and Maria watch the headlights as the vehicle turns off the main road and begins the ascent up to their plateau and runway. As the vehicle, a large SUV, reaches the top of the plateau, Xavier turns on the light under the canopy. Maria has taken up her position in the plane. The SUV pulls up to the canopy and two men get out and approach Xavier under the canopy. One of them has a very large backpack, the other man carries two very large empty duffle bags. Both men are obviously armed.

"Welcome gentlemen." Xavier says. Again, names are not used, these people are all just transporters. "Let's get this transfer started. Here's how it works. First," he says to the man with the money backpack. "Put down the money until you two verify the product. After you check it out, then I'll count the money. After that checks out, then you will pack up and leave with the product. As usual, guns are trained on you from the dark."

The two pickup men get busy verifying the product. They poke a very small hole into each package, one at a time and extract a very small sample. They rub the sample between their thumb and forefinger. They sniff it, and put a small amount into a test tube with a testing solution and shake it up and check it for the chemical reaction.

When all the packages have been verified, the head tester says, "It all checks out. This is good Columbian product."

"Okay, good, now you two return to your SUV and wait while I count the money."

The two drug runners go back to their SUV and wait. Xavier puts the money backpack on the table and opens it and begins counting the bundles of bills. These bills are not new money. It is "street money", so the bundles are irregularly bound and more difficult to count. It takes him quite a while to count it all. There is four million, five hundred and fifty six thousand dollars. He puts it all back in the backpack and walks off into the dark with it. After a few minutes, the two drug runners return to the canopy table and load the bundles of the product into the two large duffle bags and take the duffle bags back to the SUV and throw them in the back. They get in and turn the SUV around and head back down to the Bill Williams trail and to highway 95. Unbeknown to Xavier and Maria, the ‘product’ is headed to Las Vegas and will quickly be consumed over the holidays.

After Xavier and Maria see the taillights of the SUV disappear down the mountain in the distance Xavier comes out of the shadows. He turns out the light under the canopy and loads the backpack into the plane.

“Four million, five hundred and fifty six thousand, U.S. dollars,” he says to Maria, as he gets into the plane beside her.

“Boy, what we couldn’t do with that money,” she says, “A really good life in the U.S., college for the children.”

“I know,” Xavier replies, “We have this same discussion every time we do one of these runs. But, listen, Honey, that money is not ours. We will be having a very good life in the U.S. We already have a substantial amount of U.S. dollars saved from making these runs. This will be our last run, I promise, and then we can start putting together our dream life with our children in the U.S.A.”

“Okay,” she says, “You’re right, so let’s get the canopy table loaded up again, for the second pickup. Then we can put this crazy dangerous life behind us and get home to our children, they’re probably already in bed. We’ll have to wake them for Midnight Mass when we get home, but first we’ll have to put the presents under the tree that we have hidden at our airport hangar."

The rain is still coming down heavily as the two smugglers unload the second batch, this one, of twenty bundles of their product and stack it under the canopy on the table, same as for the first exchange. Then they wait again. It's about a half hour wait, and just as they are finishing having their evening lunch, they hear the plane gliding in for a landing. Xavier runs to turn on the canopy light so the runners can find the exchange spot in the blackness. There are no lights burning on this plane, same as their plane wasn't lit either. Everything happens in the absolute black darkness of this stormy night.

The plane successfully lands and taxis up to the canopy where Xavier is waiting and Maria is positioned with her rifle in their plane again, same as for the first exchange. The plane is left idling as two men get out. They each are carrying a large duffle bag, but it doesn't look like either bag would have the money in it. This sends up a red flag for both Xavier and Maria as they tense, preparing for trouble.

Before Xavier can say anything, the bigger of the two men pulls out a gun and orders Xavier to lay his gun down on the table. He does as he is told and takes his gun carefully out of his holster and lays it on the table.

"Okay," he says, "Here is what's going to happen. We're going to bag up the goods and leave with it. Any argument and you're a dead man."

Xavier doesn't realize it, but these are two mob thugs from St. Louis, where the drugs are headed. Just as the other man loads the last of the bundles into the two duffle bags, a shot rings out and the man that had the gun is no longer holding the gun. He is on the ground writhing in pain with a blown out shoulder.

"My partner is a very good shot," Xavier says.

The big guy's partner scrambles to retrieve the gun, but Xavier is faster to grabs his own gun off of the table.

"Don't even think about it," he says, "Do you think we are idiots, out here all alone in the desert in this thunder storm. I've got men behind every rock, so don't mess with me or you're dead meat. Got it? Now, I'll call the shots. Here's what's going to happen. You, the one-armed big idiot will stay here with me, while you, the little punk ass, will go back to your plane and retrieve that bag of money that I know you brought with. Don't even think about any funny maneuvers or your plane will look like Swiss cheese and you two will be hamburger. Got it?"

The little guy returns with a very large duffle-bag and Xavier has him put the money bag on the table and open it up and spread it out. Xavier can only casually look at the money because he has to have his gun trained on the two apes from St. Louis.

"Okay, now take your twenty bags of coke back to your plane along with your armless idiot here and get the hell off my mountain. I really don't want to kill you two. It creates such a mess to clean up, and we've got other customers coming in yet tonight," he lies.

The little punk grabs one bag and the big guy, with his one good arm drags the other bag to the plane. The two St. Louis mob rats get the duffle bags loaded and get in their plane and taxi it down to the far end of the runway. The rain is coming down in torrents now. Meanwhile, Xavier scoops up the money and stuffs it back into the duffle bag and runs it over to the plane and throws it in. while Maria pulls down the canopy and table and puts them in the plane. They both get in and Xavier starts the engines. He revs the engines up and attempts to pull the plane out of the mud. Just when they think it won't budge, the new heavy downpour has softened the mud. The plane leaps forward and onto the runway, just as the other plane is accelerating down the runway towards them.

Neither plane can see or hear the other because they have their lights off. The pickup plane slams into the side of Xavier and Maria's plane at about ninety miles per hour. The impact carries both planes off the runway and off the edge of the cliff and it takes with it, the transponder, not that it matters, no one will ever be listening for it again.

It is about a hundred foot drop down into the canyon, but all are dead before they hit the bottom, because the planes explode in a ball of fire on the way down. The pieces of the planes and the body parts are strewn all over the canyon floor. The bundles of the coke have likewise exploded and it snows the white powder down into the stream at the bottom of the canyon. The stream will carry it down into the Bill Williams River and then down into Lake Havasu near the dam. It will flow through the dam and down the Colorado River all the way, ironically back into Mexico.

The bags of the money, however, survive. The backpack full of money is left hanging in a Ponderosa Pine tree and the duffle bag is stuck on a rock ledge about half way down the canyon wall.

* * * * * *

And so, it ends for these drug dealers and drug transporters. It all ends here, on this rainy Christmas Eve, in this remote canyon of Arizona. The worst tragedy, perhaps, is that no one will ever know just whatever happened to these people, to Maria and Xavier and to the two mob thugs from St. Louis. There is no record of them anywhere. In this remote desert area, fifty miles from any habitation, no one probably heard or saw the planes with their lights turned off. The wreckage of their planes will not probably be found for a very long time. The tiny pieces of their exploded planes and bodies filtered down through the trees at the bottom of the canyon and will be obscured from above by the trees. The heavy rain has washed away any trace of them on their plateau runway, high above the canyon. Their body parts will be gradually consumed by the coyotes and mountain lions that call this canyon their home.

Their being there was so secret that they left no trace of this secret rendezvous. The families that they had left behind have no idea where they went for this big drug exchange. They will have no idea where to even start looking for them. To the people they left behind, they have simply vanished on this Christmas Eve, on this 'Silent Night, Holy Night.'

They are now victims of the drug war. They are now statistics, along with the thousands and tens of thousands who have foolishly given up their lives in the pursuit of drugs.

But they are not the only victims here. The real victims are the families of these people who have made such a very bad decision. Even the mob thugs probably had a family back in St. Louis.

The most painful tragedy of all, though, is the children left behind. These innocents; Xavier and Maria's children; Juanita, Madeline, Juan and Antonio will probably wake up on Christmas morning and find that their Mom and Dad are not home, nor will they ever again be coming home. They didn't wake them for Midnight Mass. There are no presents under the tree.

They won't realize right away that there will never be another Midnight Mass with their parents. Never again will there be Christmas presents from Mom and Dad under the tree. Sadly, this is the Christmas they will never forget for the rest of their lives.

The children will probably try to fix themselves some breakfast and think that Mom and Dad will be coming home at any time. After several hours, probably most of the day they will sit and wait. Finally, they will start to become very worried and will go over to a relative's house, or maybe a relative will come over. They will all wait together, all Christmas day and into the night, and the next day, and the day after that. Finally one of the adults will start to realize what may have happened. Perhaps one of the adult relatives knows what Xavier and Maria did for a living. Maybe one of the cartel people will come by and start questioning everyone about Xavier and Maria because they had not received their money.

Weeks will go by and everyone will start thinking that maybe Xavier and Maria have been arrested by the USA's FBI or the US DEA. and that they are probably in a prison somewhere in the U.S. The adult relative calls the local police and tells them what has probably happened. The local police in La Junta call the State Police, who call the Mexico equivalent of the U.S's FBI, who then call the U.S. FBI. Weeks, or months will go by before anyone hears anything. But the report comes back negative, that is, there is no record of Xavier and Maria being arrested anywhere in the US. Finally the reality will start to sink in.

Meantime, the children who have been staying with relatives, are placed in a more permanent foster home, perhaps a relative. Maybe a relative will eventually adopt them.

A very sad, sad Christmas story.

THE
DESERT BAR
HELICOPTER RIDE

There's a Christmas surprise for the snowbirds. A week before Christmas they get a call from son Chris saying he and Judy and their two girls, Elizabeth and Louise will be flying out for Christmas. Mike and Audrey head up to Las Vegas to pick them up for their three day holiday stay. There's a big party provided by their condo association, with plenty of food and drink. After the party they all attend the traditional Christmas Midnight Mass. These visits are always way too short, and it's back to Vegas with the kids and grandkids to catch the flight back to 'snowy' Minnesota. Promises are made by all of them to get together again next summer in Minnesota.

* * * * **

As the snow is coming down heavily in Northern Minnesota, in a New Year's Eve blizzard, Mike and Audrey's driveway at their lake house is now buried under two feet of snow. But, don't tell them about it. They don't know about it and they won't want to hear about it. This is the exact reason that they are here; in sunny Arizona, and they are in the mood for some New Year's Eve fun and partying.

At their Saturday night card get-together just before New Year's, the three couples discuss plans for New Year's Eve.

"Well, we could get together at our condo complex," Mike says, "They're having a big party."

"Yeah," Audrey continues, "It's going to be a pool party. They have a heated indoor pool."

"Well, we have a pool at our house," Bill says, "But, it's not heated yet. The solar heating is just not effective this time of year."

"And, it's outdoors," Mia adds, "And it's just too cold this time of year."

"Oh, you Arizonians are always freezing this time of year," Audrey quips, "This sixty and seventy degrees you have here is probably our average summertime temperature in Minnesota."

"Yeah, yeah," Rick interrupts, "Whatever - enough with the temperature talk. You displaced Minnesotans are all weather addicts, always talking about the weather, no matter where you go. Here's something else to talk about. I hear they are opening up the Desert Bar for the season, on New Year's Eve."

"Now, that sounds like a plan," Rhonda adds, "I love that place, it's so, so unique."

"Let's go, then," Bill agrees, "The only thing is; they close early, usually at sundown because they don't have electricity way out there in the desert."

"Why don't we go out there until they close, then join the pool party at our condo," Mike concludes.

"Okay, it's all set then," Audrey adds. "Who's driving?"

"I'll drive." Rick volunteers, "We have that big suburban we can all fit into. our place at one o'clock, then."

* * * * *

December thirty first, at one, P.M. The Desert Bar is located, well, - - - -, out in the desert, about three miles southeast off of highway 95, just north of Parker, Arizona. The turn-off is easy enough to miss and the road in is a dirt and rock road, all the way into the bar. The road has been just bulldozed through the rugged terrain. There are huge boulders pushed up alongside the road. In most places it's a single lane road and drivers have to wait their turn to get to a place to pass oncoming vehicles. Huge rocks and boulders sticking up in the roadway are the norm, as are sharp turns and really steep hills. Not the road for a low-slung sedan. Four-wheel drive SUV types are way more appropriate.

Rick maneuvers his Suburban carefully and slowly through the obstacles. The trip of about three miles takes about a half hour. At the end of the road, they end up in a "bowl" shaped valley with the bar complex at the end of the bowl. They first have to pass through the gateway, which is a narrow passage between two very huge boulders, one on either side of the road, then up to the parking lot which sits on a small rocky plateau. Below the parking lot lies the bar.

At the edge of the parking lot, situated on a rocky rise is a very strange looking structure that is the hallmark of the bar. It is what at first appears to be the front wall of a church. (It may have been an actual church at one time). But it is just a large wall with a gothic type door in the middle and a gothic window on either side of the 'church' door.

Up on the opposite side of the bowl shaped canyon, higher up on the hillside, there are remnants of several mining structures from ancient gold or silver mines. There are rumors that some of them are still actively mined. A short wooden walking bridge over a small narrow canyon connects the parking lot to the main part of the bar. The bar was also once an active gold mine. The bar is situated on three different levels. The main level has two structures made entirely of corrugated metal, some galvanized, some not. One of the structures houses the main bar. The other one has a walkup food counter. The food, mostly burgers and pizza has to be brought in pre-cooked. There is no electricity at the bar. This is why they have to close at sundown. A small patio area with umbrella tables lies between the two buildings. There is an upper area, above the food building, and a lower seating area down below everything on the canyon floor, also with umbrella tables. A band stand is situated alongside the food bar and elevated above the patio. The electricity for the band instruments is provided by a generator.

As you walk up a rocky trail above the bar, up over a ridge, you can see down into another parking area in a small valley. This one is for four-wheeler ATV's. Rising up on the other side of the parking area on a small flat topped rocky plateau is the helicopter landing pad. They offer sight-seeing rides around the area. The canyons and high sheer cliffs rising above Lake Havasu and the Colorado River below the dam are quite spectacular, as well as the Bill Williams river valley all the way up to Alamo Lake; especially viewed from above.

The group finds a large table. They each go up to the bar and get the drink of their choice and they all settle in to enjoy some great music provided by the Desert Rats, a country – pop style band. After a couple hours and several beers later, the guys are getting restless.

Bill says, "We should try the helicopter ride. I took it last winter. It's very spectacular."

"I'm game for it," Mike says, "How about any of you gals?"

"Nah," Mia replies, "I went last year with Bill. I think I'll give someone else a chance this year."

"Not me," Audrey says, "I don't think I trust helicopters."

"Me either," Rhonda says, "You guys go ahead, we'll just wait here, safely on the ground."

"I think I'll let you two go, "Rick says, "I've been up several times in the past, and it's kind of pricy and they can only take two at a time "

With that, Mike and Bill walk up the trail to get their tickets. The helicopters are quite busy, they find out, and they have a wait time of half hour, so they return to the table and have another beer.

At about four P.M. the two tourists return to the helicopter pad and present their tickets. They get in and buckle themselves in. The chopper lifts off and the pilot says, "Welcome aboard. I'm Captain Wilson. Hope you enjoy the ride. Have you guys ever flown in a helicopter, or "Chopper" before?"

"I have," Bill says, "I was here and flew with you last spring. Before that, I made a lot of trips in Vietnam a very long time ago."

"I've flown before as well, "Mike says, "When I was in the Army, way back in the Sixties, half way across the globe from Nam. I was stationed at the Army's Arctic test facility in Alaska. I had to deliver courier documents of test results all around Alaska at their test sites."

"Okay, it looks like we've all had flying experience in the Military. I was a chopper pilot in Afghanistan. with too many missions to count, but the terrain here, I find very similar. Well, here's our flight pattern for today. We're going to fly over the Parker area and the Parker Dam, then head up the lake a ways to the Copper Canyon area on the California side. From there, we'll cut back across the lake to where the Bill Williams River flows into the lake and follow the river all the way to its source at Alamo Lake. We'll return back here by flying over the Buckskin Mountain area."

They cut over to Parker to see the dam from above, then up the lake just a little way, on the California side to see the largest pumping station on the Colorado River. It pushes water from the lake, up and over a mountain ridge through water pipes that are large enough to drive a car through. The water is then dumped into an aqueduct that carries the water all the way across the California Mohave Desert to Los Angeles. Up the western shore of the lake a couple miles is the Copper Canyon. The pilot brings the chopper right down into the canyon for a very spectacular sight.

Back across the lake, they pick up the Bill Williams River and begin following it upstream through beautiful gorges and rocky cliffs. They make a loop around Alamo Lake. As they are cutting back across the Buckskin Mountains, they fly over a deep canyon that feeds into the river. The canyon is filled with a lot of foliage, but just as they are crossing it, Mike and Bill see just a sudden glint of the late afternoon sun reflecting off something down in the canyon, mostly hidden by the trees and brush on the canyon floor. It flashes, just for a second, then; it's gone as the chopper skims on rapidly over the canyon. They are just about to mention it, but it was just a flash, then it disappeared again. They don't say anything, but that flash sticks in their minds. It's like, almost forgotten as they fly up and over the Buckskin Mountains, then down into the valley, and the Desert Bar to the landing pad. But, that flash will stay stuck in the back of their minds.

Mike and Bill rejoin Rick, Ronda, Mia and Audrey, all of whom are still sitting on the main patio enjoying the music.

“So, how was your chopper tour,” Audrey asks.

“Oh, it was fabulous. The view from up above all this canyon land is so spectacular. You should go sometime.”

They all decide they are hungry, but don’t want to buy dinner at the Bar when they can get free food at the pool party at Audrey and Mike’s condo. So, they head back down the rocky, dusty, dirt road back to the highway and head north to Lake Havasu City and their New Year’s Eve pool party.

BALLOONS, SNAKES FISH

Mid-January in Lake Havasu, means the Annual Balloon Festival. The view from Mike and Audrey's balcony is spectacular. About fifty hot air balloons of many brilliant colors and various shapes and sizes are sent up from the Lake Havasu Island. They float about a hundred feet above them as a light breeze carries them slowly up and down Lake Havasu. Eventually the breeze carries them up into the city, riding up the mountain on the thermal breezes, where they descend down onto pre-arranged landing zones all around the residential areas of town..

They have invited their friends, Bill and Mia to join them for the viewing. Even though it's Mid-January, the temperature is in the sixties, so they are all dressed in shorts and polo or tank tops. They all enjoy a great meal on the balcony, followed by an evening of playing cards and enjoying drinks. Bill talks about the fishing trip he has planned for the four of them, down to the Copper Canyon area for some Striper fishing.

"I will be freed up, probably late next week, how about we say the twenty second of the month?"

"Sounds okay by us," Audrey says, "That sounds very exciting. Actually, we haven't been fishing on Lake Havasu in several years. After the DNR raised the price of temporary fishing permits, it's just been too expensive to go fishing. We'll have to be sure to get our 'out-of-state', temporary fishing permits by then.

* * * * * *

January twenty second at four thirty in the morning, Mike and Audrey meet the Wilson's at their house. It's a very chilly morning with a temperature of only about fifty something. The dry desert air cools down a lot at night. The Wilsons have on layered clothing, long pants and winter jackets, as well gloves and caps with ear-flaps. The Felders also have on layers of clothing and their 'Minnesota' parkas.

Mia says, "Glad you guys dressed in warm layers. It gets really cold out on the lake this time of year."

"Yeah," Bill adds, "The water temperature is still in the forties, and with a Northwest wind blowing across that cold water, it chills you to the bone.."

"Still better then Minnesota in January," Mike states, "The temp is in the teens and twenty below zero. When you go fishing, you drive your vehicle out onto the ice, drill a hole and fish right alongside of your vehicle. The ice is about thirty inches thick this time of the winter."

"And, that's exactly why we live here now," Mia responds.

"Okay, now that we've got the weather issues taken care of," Bill says, "We should get going. The stripers hit best right at sun-up"

Bill gets the boat hooked up and they head down to the lake and launch the boat at the Windsor boat ramp. There is just the faintest glimmer of daylight starting to show from behind Crossman Mountain as they all pile into the boat, along with all the fishing gear and lunches and make their way down-lake to the Copper Canyon area.

The stripers start to hit their bait as soon as they can get them into the water. The bait they use is cut-up anchovies. By nine A.M., some of them have filled out their limit of four stripers. Bill and Mia, of course are real 'pro's' at it. Audrey has three and Mike, two. So Bill gets out his cleaning board and begins cleaning what they've caught so far and gets them into the cooler, on ice. They fish for about another hour, but no further stripers are caught.

"That's so typical of the striper," Bill says, "They feed so voraciously in the early morning, but when they are done, they're done. They will quit biting just as abruptly as they have started."

"Well, I don't know about the rest of you," Mia says, "But, I'm starved. What say we head in and get some breakfast."

"Sounds good to me," Bill says as he pulls up the anchor. They head further down the lake to the town of Parker. There, they find a dock-side restaurant right on the waterfront.

At breakfast, while the girls head to the bathroom, Mike says to Bill, "Have you ever thought any more about that glint of sunlight that we saw down in that canyon from the helicopter, back on New Years?"

"Yes, I have," Bill replies, "I think we should head up there and check it out. I think we should go this afternoon. We should have time. The fish aren't biting anymore anyway."

When the girls get back, Mike and Bill discuss with them, doing a little exploring up the Bill Williams River.

"Sure," Mia agrees, "That sounds like fun."

"As long as there are no snakes up there," Audrey says, "I hate snakes."

"Don't we all?" Bill says, "I make no promises."

"I haven't seen a snake in Arizona in all the years we've been coming here," Mike says.

After breakfast, they all get back in the boat and head over to the mouth of the Bill Williams River, which is just a little ways from Parker.

Bill carefully navigates the boat up the river.

"This river is usually not navigable ," Mia says, "But with the high water we have this year after all the rain we've had, maybe we can get up the river a ways."

They get up the river about a mile when the river becomes more shallow and very rocky.

"Looks like that's as far as we can go, "Bill says, "I don't want to wreck the prop or damage the hull. I'll pull over to shore. Maybe we can hike for a ways. I think there's a trail that follows the river."

Bill secures the boat and they all get out and take their lunches with. They shed their winter jackets because it's quite a bit warmer away from the cold lake water. After hiking for about a mile, they decide to stop and eat their lunch. Just as Mike is about to sit down on a large rock alongside the trail, he hears a kind of rattling, hissing sound. Even before he sees the snake, he feels a very sharp pain in his lower leg on his shin. He howls out in pain as the snake slithers away, but coils for another strike. They all come running over to see what is the matter.

Mike yells out, “Dammit, I’ve been bit,” as he points to the snake a few feet away. Bill grabs up a large rock and slams it down on the snake.

Audrey says, “Where did it get you?”

“Here, on my shin,” Mike says as he pulls up his pant leg.

“Looks like it hit you mostly right on your shin bone,“ Audrey says, “So his fangs probably didn’t penetrate very deep”.

“Here, let’s see if we can get as much of the venom out as we can,” Mia says as she peels off her sweatshirt. She puts pressure just beneath the bite and dabs out some of the venom that she squeezes out into her sweatshirt.

“I’ve got a snake-bite kit in the boat,” Bill says, “I’ll run back and get it. You just lie down and try to completely relax to slow down your circulation and slow down the venom from spreading.”

As Bill takes off running back to the boat, Mike lays flat on the ground and tries to totally relax. Bill returns in about a half hour and Audrey administers the anti-venom shot into Mike’s thigh. They wait about fifteen minutes for the anti-venom to get into Mike’s system, then get him up and help him hobble down the trail to the boat. They have to make several stops along the way so Mike can sit down and let his leg stop throbbing.

Finally they get back to the boat where Audrey has cell service again and she calls 911 and sets up for an ambulance to meet them at the mouth of the river at the highway ninety-95 bridge. Once in the ambulance, they monitor his vitals on the way to the hospital. Audrey, Mia and Bill have to take the boat back to the Havasu landing. They then head to the hospital where Mike is now stable and the doctor says he can probably go home later that night. The doctor says for him to stay off that leg for a couple of days.

"Well, so much for exploring," Mike says, "Maybe we'll have a chance to go again in a week or so."

"I don't know," Bill says, "I'm booked up solid, now through most of February."

"Maybe Audrey and I can go again by ourselves, later. I am really anxious to explore that canyon that we saw from that helicopter ride."

"Well, not until we get ourselves a snake-bite kit," Audrey says. Later that evening, after Mike is checked out of the hospital they head for their CRV in the parking lot, Audrey notices a very large pool of oil under their car.

"Oh, oh," Audrey says what's that?"

"That looks like engine oil that has leaked out from under our CRV. I think that maybe we have somehow punctured our oil pan from driving all those rough roads when we're out exploring. Well, we can't drive it like this, and it's too late to get it into a shop tonight."

"Here, I'll call a cab to get us home."

The next morning, they call around for a car repair shop and a tow truck. However, they find that no one in Havasu has a shop that can repair or replace a CRV oil pan. The nearest Honda dealer is in Kingman, Arizona. Mike calls them and makes arrangements to get the CRV into their shop. More bad news, however. It could take weeks, or up to a month to get a new oil pan in. Mike calls a tow truck to pick up their CRV and tow it to the Honda dealer in Kingman, Arizona, about sixty miles away.

Audrey calls their triple 'A' motor club to find out about getting a rental car while waiting for their Honda. Enterprise soon arrives with a rental, another CRV for them to drive.

SOJOURN INTO DARKNESS

By the end of February, the winter rains are over and many of the desert plants are starting to bloom. The 'Arizona famous' Saguaro cactus with its large white blooms is Arizona's state flower. Also blooming, are Arizona's many other cacti. The Prickly Pear has large round pink or yellow blooms. The Barrel cactus has brilliant orange flowers. The long 'stick-like' Ocotillo grows mostly in clusters and has elongated orange flowers. The Teddy Bear cactus doesn't have flowers exactly, but rather, produces thousands of the fuzzy white needles. The Aloe Vera, not truly a cactus, blooms with spindly orange elongated petals. These and hundreds of other cactus species bloom from February through May.

Most all of the other hundreds of desert plants are also in bloom this time of year. The creosote bush produces hundreds of small, bright yellow flowers. The climbing Bougainvillea vines and bushes produce brilliant crimson red blooms.

Mike and Audrey have limited themselves to walking along the Havasu channel, every day, because of Mike's snake-bit leg. The time passes all too quickly and it is soon time to welcome the next onslaught of tourists to Lake Havasu. It's Spring Break for school kids and college students. The spring-breakers descend on the lakeside resort city. Spring-breakers from Minnesota, Mike and Audrey's daughter Linda and grand-daughter Betsey arrive, along with her fiance Bruce. It's a fun-filled week for them, basking in the warm Arizona sun and boating and swimming in the lake along with the comradery and partying of the thousands of spring-breakers. All too soon, it's over and back to reality. It's back to the books for all these partyers. Mike and Audrey's spring-breakers are packed and ready. However Linda has reservations about flying back. She has a fear of flying, so Audrey suggests maybe she could drive the Honda CRV back to Minnesota, along with their cat, Maggie. She and Mike have just gotten word that the car's oil-pan has finally been replaced. She suggests that she and Mike could just drive the rental car back, later. So they drive the kids up to Kingman and send them off in their Honda.

* * * * *

But now, with his leg completely healed, these two snowbirds are ready for some more adventure. Mike has been really anxious to get back out to the Bill Williams Trail and search for that canyon again. Their friends, Bill and Mia are tied up with their jobs; Bill with his fishing guide service on the lake. and Mia volunteering at the library and hospital. This is the busy time of year for Lake Havasu City. With the thousands of snowbirds in town, the permanent residents are kept hopping to fulfill their needs and take their money.

"Well, looks like we'll be on our own, this trip," Mike says, "Looks like our friends will be pretty tied up for the rest of the winter."

"Yeah," agrees Audrey, "They're so busy, they're having a tough time just finding time for our card night every week. It looks like it's just you and I for this next adventure."

"So, let's get out our hiking gear again and get going in the morning."

Very early the next morning, they start packing for the hike. They've made sure their cell phones have been fully charged. They pack a lunch and fill a backpack with lots of bottled water, and of course their snake-bite kit and a compass. Mike also puts his hunting knife on his belt. They get on their hiking boots and sweatshirts for the early morning chill, jeans and tee shirts for when the day warms up.

"Well, I think we've got everything," Audrey says as they load it all in their rental SUV.

"Not quite," Mike adds, as he grabs their two walking sticks from the corner of the garage and tosses them in.

On their way out of town, they gas up the rented CRV and stop at a McDonald's and pick up Egg Mc Muffins and coffee for breakfast, to eat on the road. The trip down to the Bill Williams Recreation area and trail is about eighteen miles. Mike finds the trail entrance and turns up the trail.

"Whoa," Audrey says as they get to where the trail goes right along the river, "Looks like the trail gets real muddy here, down along the river."

Soon the trail rises up above the river and the trail is dry again, albeit, quite rocky as they navigate over the rocks and up and down sharp hills and curves, and through very narrow passage ways through the thick willow trees.

"You know, it's really quite scenic on this trail, with all the hills and valleys and the river down below with all its foliage," Mike comments.

"Yeah, but I sure wouldn't want to be down this trail without four-wheel drive."

Soon, they pass the spot on the trail, of the infamous snake incident. Mike cringes as they pass by. "Sure as heck hope we don't see any more of those snake creatures on this trip," he says.

"I hope not, too, that must have been pretty painful for you."

About a half mile further, they come to a tee where a trail comes in from the south, out of the Buckskin Mountains and merges with the Bill Williams Trail for a couple hundred yards.

(Unbeknownst to Mike and Audrey, that was the trail that the drug runners used to get up to that plateau for the drug exchange, back on Christmas Eve. But they don't follow it.)

The trail drops down again, to the river, to a spot where the other trail breaks off and crosses the river. There is no bridge there, but the river is very shallow at the crossing. They are thankful they don't have to cross the river. As they push on down the trail a little further, they come to where the trail virtually ends in a very large muddy swamp.

"Well, it looks like this is as far as we can go in the CRV," Mike says. as he parks their vehicle in a small parking area above the swamp.

They get out and get their hiking supplies out of the back. Mike puts on the backpack and they both pick up their walking sticks and head out across the swamp following the narrow hiking trail for almost a mile. About half way across the swamp, they come to a small creek. They look up the creek and see that it flows out of the mouth of a very deep canyon. High up above the canyon, they see a flat topped plateau and beyond that the jagged peaks of the Buckskin Mountains.

"I think this is the canyon that we're looking for," Mike says.

"It looks like a jungle up in there," Audrey says, "There's no telling what we'll find."

"I know, right, that's the fun of exploring. We'll be okay as long as there are no snakes up in that canyon."

Mike digs in the backpack and gets out the compass and a map. He takes a reading on the compass. "Looks like that canyon runs pretty much north and south from this trail which runs east and west. The canyon and this creek however, are not shown on the map."

"Wow," Audrey says, "It looks like we're heading into uncharted territory. How exciting is this. I just hope we don't get lost up in that canyon and in those mountains. Also, there's no telling what kind of wildlife we'll run into up in that canyon."

The two explorers push on, through the tall swamp grass alongside the small creek for about a half mile and come to the mouth of the canyon. They find a dry spot above the creek.

"Well, let's have some lunch," Audrey said, "It's already well past one o'clock."

They sit on the grassy knoll to rest for a while after the hike and ate their lunch. As they proceeded up into the canyon, the creek becomes steeper and rockier than it was back down in the swamp. The water now tumbled over the rocks in small rivulets. The banks of the creek are now covered with thick brush and large rocks and boulders, making it difficult to navigate and very slow going. Fortunately, after a short distance, the brush gave way to an area of very tall trees with a thick canopy, inhibiting the growth of the brush.

"Well, that was quite a struggle," Mike said as they paused for a rest and a drink, "I think the way will get easier now, without all that brush to struggle through."

After their break, the two snowbird explorers push on again, up into the canyon. They noticed that the sides of the canyon are becoming taller and more cliff-like. Mike notices another small trail that follows along the creek.

"This one has obviously been used by animals," he points out to Audrey.

"See here, there are coyote tracks," Mike explains, "They probably follow the creek way back up in the canyon, looking for food, like rabbits or quail, or road-runners."

"Oh, look," Audrey says, "See those cat-like tracks. Are those mountain lion tracks? I want to leave now, please Mike. Let's go back now. Haven't we seen enough?"

"No, wait now, Audrey. Those are very small cat-like tracks. Probably just a small bobcat, I'm sure it couldn't hurt us."

"Okay, but I'm becoming nervous about this. It's too bad you didn't bring a gun."

"Well, as you know, I don't own a handgun and all my hunting rifles are back in Minnesota. We'll just have to tough it through without any weaponry."

As they follow the creek further into the canyon, Audrey spots something of interest in the creek, hung up on one of the rocks.

"Oh look, it looks like a piece of fabric, or a piece of clothing," she says as she picks it off of the rock and looks at it in detail. "It looks like a woman's sweater, a bright red sweater. How in the world do you suppose this got there? Has someone else already explored this canyon?"

"Maybe there's a campsite up ahead that will explain that," Mike says.

Audrey spreads the sweater out on a large boulder to dry, for no apparent reason, as they pick up their walking sticks and continue up the canyon. The canyon now has walls that are about thirty to fifty feet high. The tall trees with their canopies continue to grow up from the canyon floor. Along the creek there are willows, and now there is a mix of the ponderosa pine mixed in with the deciduous trees. It now seems like it is somewhat darker under the thick canopy, until they look up through tiny spaces between the trees and see a sky now clouding up and darkening the canyon even more.

They move further into the canyon and suddenly discover more articles of clothing scattered all around on the ground. There is a man's boot and further along, a man's plaid red shirt and a jacket all ripped to shreds.

"I wonder what the hell is going on here," Mike comments.

Audrey just shakes her head and mutters, "This is all very strange and weird. I wonder what lies up ahead."

They push further on up the canyon. Now they see pieces of metal scattered around along with pieces of plastic. As they move into the deeper part of the canyon the canyon walls are now about a hundred feet high and the air becomes stagnant.

"What's that smell?" Audrey asks.

"I think it's the smell of perhaps a dead animal. Maybe the coyotes have left something of their kill behind."

But that proves to not be the case, as they move further along and see more metal shapes scattered around. inter-mixed with some tree branches. Some of the metal shapes began making sense. Suddenly it becomes apparent what had happened here.

Audrey says, almost in a whisper, "Mike, I think we've just come upon an airplane crash site."

This is totally confirmed to them as they begin to find bones, lots of bones, scattered everywhere across a very wide area. No flesh on them, just the bones. The ground in this area is all torn up, like some sort of struggle.

"I think the coyotes have gotten to them," Mike says. The crash must have happened quite a while ago." As they come upon a skeleton head stripped clean of its flesh, then another. They count four in all, scattered among the shredded pieces of the airplane. Some of the pieces of the plane are quite large and easily recognized. A broken propeller here and there, and pieces of the wings scattered over the whole area. There are plane seat pieces, and pieces of the planes dashboards lying everywhere.

"Oh. look," Mike says, "Here's a planes' door, pretty much in tact leaning up against a rock with its window unbroken. I'll bet this is what we saw, reflecting in the sun, from that helicopter ride last New Year's. My guess is that there were two planes involved here, judging from the number of like plane parts. Perhaps a mid-air collision. The planes parts and body parts just rained down through the trees"

There are bits and pieces of fabric and cords and wires hanging from the trees.

"We should get out of here," Audrey says, "This needs to be checked out by the NTSB."

But, just as she says that, they hear the rumble of thunder from above the canyon.

"We better find shelter," Mike says, "And on higher ground in case there's a flash flood down on this canyon floor."

They run to the canyon wall and climb up to a ledge where there is an overhang of rock to keep them out of the rain. They hear more thunder that echoes loudly down in the canyon, as flashes of lightning light up the whole area.

"This is going to be a really heavy storm, and this overhang is just not enough protection."

Mike looks around and further up the ledge, on a wide spot he sees a fairly large piece of the plane. It's one of the tail sections, lodged into the rocks at the side of the ledge. They climb up to the tail section and Mike checks the inside for any critters that may have made a home in it.

"Make sure there are no spiders or snakes in there," Audrey says, "Also, most importantly, no human body parts, or bones."

"Nope, none of the above," he says."

They crawl into it as the canyon goes very dark and the rain pours down and the thunder is deafening as it rolls down into the canyon and the lightning lights up the floor of the canyon. The deluge of rain continues for over an hour. Suddenly they hear another thunder-like roar. As they look down into the canyon, lit up from the flashes of the lightning, they see a huge wall of murky water come rushing down the canyon floor. The small canyon creek that they had followed into the canyon had become a huge torrent of a river, a flash flood, carrying with it a lot of the wreckage and also burying a lot of the bones of the poor souls killed in the mid-air collision high above the canyon in the silt and sand that was carried down the canyon by the torrent of water.

"This will probably be the only burial that they will get," sighs Audrey. "I'm so thankful we found this ledge high enough above all that water. We would have drown and our bodies swept down the creek along with some of those bones, probably all the way down to the Bill Williams river."

After a while though, the heavy part of the storm passes and the rain becomes somewhat lighter, but persists on into the evening as darkness descends.

THE BACKPACK FROM HELL

"Could we go soon?" Audrey asks, "I don't think I want to spend the night with all those dead people lying around down there."

"Well, I'm afraid we'll be doing just that," Mike says as he checks his lit dial watch, "It's already almost nine o'clock. I don't want to attempt to navigate that trail back to the car in the dark with the creek probably still swollen and that mucky flooded swamp to cross. At least we'll be dry in here and up off the floor of the canyon where the coyotes run around all night. We should be safe and comfortable here for the night."

They try to get comfortable for the night. The tail section of the plane still has the rear seat intact, so they fold it down into a bed. They still have four bottles of water left in their backpack, along with a couple of granola bars. So they have two for their supper. They also have their sweatshirts in the backpack from the early morning start on their adventure. They put those back on and try to get comfortable in the icy dampness after the cold rain

"Oh, this is all way too creepy," Audrey says, "It's like spending the night in a cemetery."

After a long while, they finally fall into a restless sleep, trying not to think about all those body parts and bones down below. In the middle of the night they are awakened by the howling and yipping of the coyotes down below as they still forage for some food among all the bones. The two adventurers feel safe on their ledge fairly high above the canyon bottom. They fall back into their restless sleep, but wake up several more times before daylight finally comes creeping down into the cold and damp, dark canyon.

"What's for breakfast, Honey," Mike says as they crawl back out of the plane's fuselage tail section. "Just kidding."

"Oh, very funny Mike, all we have is some water left." as she transfers the last two bottles into her pack, and leaves the other pack in the plane. Let's just please get out of here and let those peoples bones rest in peace. I'll be having nightmares about this place, probably for the rest of my life. It's like we're in a creepy horror movie, - - - - and we've just spent the night in a cemetery."

They both stand there on the ledge and look out over the scene down below in the morning twilight.

Mike says, “This looks like a scene from Hell.”

“Or a battlefield scene in a war with all this destruction,” Audrey says.

”Be careful, Honey, as you climb down from the ledge,” Mike warns as they both scramble off of their ledge bedroom.

As Audrey climbs down and partially slides down, from the ledge, she hits a large rock near the bottom with her left foot and jams her foot into the rock. She cries out in pain, as Mike scrambles quickly over to her side.

“What happened, Honey, are you all right?”

“Oh no, I think I just twisted my ankle. The same one that I broke that time I climbed down from that dry falls north of Havasu.”

“Do you think it’s broken again?” Mike asks.

“No, it doesn’t feel broken, just sprained, but It hurts like heck. I don’t think I’ll be able to walk on it.”

“Here, sit down on the rock and I’ll see if I can rig up a crutch for you to walk with, so we can get the heck out of here. I think this place is cursed, - - - - or haunted, - - - or both. Anyway, let me have your walking stick. What we need to do is find a piece of wood and attach it, in the shape of a tee, to the top of your stick."

"Well, there are still plenty of tree branches lying around," she says.

As Mike picks up a short piece of a broken branch and gets out his knife and begins fashioning a top piece for Audrey's crutch, they both look up in the trees where the branches have been broken off by the airplane and body parts that came raining down. "Oh, look, what's that hanging up there, amongst all the debris suspended from tree branches?"

"I see it," Mike says, "It looks like some sort of backpack."

"Maybe it's a parachute pack," Audrey says, "If so, it's too bad someone couldn't have used it;"

"I'm going to climb up there and see what it is," Mike says as he finishes fashioning the top piece of the crutch and attaches it with a piece of the wire cable he found lying around, "Here, try that on for size"

"Oh, thank you, this will work perfectly. Now you be careful climbing up there. We don't need both of us crippled up for the trek back to our car."

Mike begins climbing the tree and finds it pretty easy going. The tree is a large ponderosa pine that has grown up at an angle, and has a lot of branches close to the ground for great handholds. The branches that had been broken off by the plane parts luckily left branch stubs for hand and foot holds. The pack is about twenty feet off the ground, but Mike easily climbs up to it. He struggles though, to get it down.

"This pack is really heavy and it's a very large backpack," He reports back down to Audrey, "I think it's waterlogged from all the rain last night."

Finally, he frees it and drops it to the ground with a heavy thud, as he climbs back down.

"I just hope it contains something interesting, instead of just someone's clothing or something, for all your trouble," she says.

"Well, we are about to find out," he says as he drags it over and places it on a flat topped rock next to Audrey and begins to unzip it.

They both just stare into the large backpack in total shock and amazement - - - - - -, it is filled with money. Lots and lots of money, all banded together into bundles, hundreds, maybe thousands of bundles.

"O-M-G, I can't believe what I am seeing," Audrey says.

"Holy crap," Mike says, his mind racing and processing, "I believe we've stumbled onto a huge drug deal gone bad. These bills, are all used bills, as in drug money. The backpack and money are all very wet and soggy from all the rain and we certainly don't have time to stop and count it now."

"But, where is it from, - - -, and how, and did I hear you say that we are going to keep all this money?"

"Well, of course. No one else is ever going to find it. It's been here for months already. It will just lie here in the weather and rot away. It's basically illegal money and the people who obtained it illegally are all obviously dead. We may as well keep it for ourselves and put it to good use. Right?"

"Well, I suppose you're right, but it just doesn't feel right yet, getting money that we haven't earned, and somehow it feels like we're robbing from the dead."

"Okay, let's see if we can figure this out. Here's what I think. I noticed that the tail section of the plane that we slept in last night had some kind of insignia imprinted on the side of it. It had some lettering that was in Spanish, maybe a drug cartel symbol. My guess is that one of the planes was headed back into Mexico with this drug money. It was probably being pursued by the other plane, maybe an FBI plane or The Border Patrol, when they collided over this canyon, maybe in a thunder storm. Both planes were probably flying blind, and without any registered flight plans."

(*Not a bad guess, Mike, albeit wrong. But probably close enough, seeing as how nobody will ever know the true story.*)

"But why haven't they been found? This crash site has obviously been here for a while."

"Well, look up at the canopy of the trees, Honey. Even if the drug cartel or the FBI had done a search from the air, they wouldn't have been able to see the crash site through the tree canopy. It was just a lucky fluke that Bill and I spotted that reflection from our helicopter ride.

"Well, we better get the heck out of here, before someone else finds this place, - - - - and us, if we don't get out of here."

"Why don't you just rest that ankle a bit longer while I quickly look around some more."

"Okay, but please, please hurry up, I'm getting very nervous and scared about this whole thing."

Mike hurriedly scouted around the crash site. He finds some of the guns scattered around, but lets them be. He also comes across several of the drug packages, wrapped in plastic, half buried in the mud, with a white powder inside. This pretty well confirms his theory about the drug money on the plane.

"But, why would there be drug money and the drugs both, on the plane going back to Mexico?" Audrey asks.

"A very good question," Mike says, "That is a mystery that may never be solved. At least, not today. Okay, I've seen enough. Let's get out of this "hell-on-earth" place."

"Oh thank God," Audrey says as she gets to her feet and gets the crutch comfortably under her arm, "I thought we'd never get going. It's going to be slow going, with me hobbling on my crutch and you with this very heavy backpack of very soggy money."

Mike zips the backpack up again and struggles to get it on his shoulders. He has to make several adjustments to the straps to get it to fit him, but he finally gets it comfortable and they began hobbling back towards the trail that will take them out of the canyon and down the trail to their SUV. Audrey was right, it was slow going, not so much across the canyon floor, which is fairly level, albeit very muddy still from the flash flood. They slowly make their way back over to the creek. But, climbing back down along the creek as it exits the canyon is a real struggle for them both, Audrey with her sprained ankle and Mike with the heavy, soggy backpack.

They finally reach the grassy knoll at the edge of the swamp and take a break. It's now almost noon. They have the last of their water and continue along the creek and across the very muddy swamp. The going gets tough again, with their handicaps, getting through the thick brush along the creek. Finally they come to the mouth of the creek where it dumps into the Bill Williams River. Here they pick up the river trail and head west. Finally, it's much easier hiking. Soon they get to the parking area and their CRV and collapse into it, totally exhausted from the hike out of the canyon and not getting much sleep in the tail section of that drug plane.

* * * * * *

In a short while, they fall sound asleep. They do not hear the sound of another vehicle pulling into the rocky parking area at the end of the road. Sometime later they are suddenly awakened by someone rapping on the driver's side window. Mike slowly opens his eyes and opens his window. The middle-aged man, dressed in an all-green uniform introduces himself.

"Hi, My name is Edward Diggeles, I'm a Park Ranger here in Buckskin Mountain State Park. May I see some identification."

Mike surrenders his driver s license.

"From Minnesota," The Ranger says, "snowbirds, I take it?"

"Yes sir, that's correct."

"Whatcha' doin' out here?"

"Well, sir, we just hiked back from doing some camping up at Alamo Lake," Mike lied.

"Well that's quite a hike, at your age, no wonder you're taking a snooze. Do you know, there's no sleeping overnight in the park?"

"No, sir, I did not know that. And I didn't realize that we were actually in the Park. I didn't see any signs on the road coming in here."

"Well, that's kind of a tricky situation for newcomers. Back at the highway where this road comes in, you're not in the Park. It's just this one little loop in through here that crosses into park territory. That's why there's no sign. So, technically you can't park here without a park permit. Say, that's quite a backpack you have in the back, there. I might have to take a look in it. Do you folks have any firearms with you?"

"No sir, we do not."

"I had to ask. I get a lot of, mostly young people that come in here and shoot the place up, and that's a danger to everyone else, that's why it's illegal to have a firearm in a state park."

"Well we don't own a pistol and all my hunting rifles are back in Minnesota."

"Did you know you fell asleep with your tail gate open?"

"No sir, I didn't realize it. We were pretty exhausted when we got back, and our backpack just has camping gear in it."

"Well, you folks have a great day. You seem like real nice snowbirds. Sorry if it seemed like I was hassling you. I'm just trying to do my job, ya know. You rest up a bit before you head out. This road can be a bit tricky."

When the Ranger left, Mike got out and closed the tailgate and got back in.

"O M G," Audrey said, "I was just about to "Mess my pants". What if he had opened the backpack? Let's just get the heck out of here."

Mike waited a while until the ranger was out of sight, back down the road, then he slowly started down the river road back to the highway.

* * * * **

But now new problems come to light.

"I'm getting really worried," Audrey says, "About transporting all this money. What if we get stopped for a traffic violation? We'll go to jail for having all this illegal money. And what if we have an accident? What do we do with the money, and how do we process it?"

As Mike begins heading back down the very rugged road back to the highway, they begin discussing their options.

"I think we'll have to get a storage locker to keep the money in until we can get it into a bank account somewhere," Mike says.

"First," Audrey says, "we'll have to somehow dry it out. Then, can't we just put it into our bank accounts?"

"Well, we can put some of it into our personal accounts, but not very much of it. Depending on how much there is. I'm guessing maybe tens of thousands of dollars. The problem is that too big of a deposit sends up a red flag for the banks and they have to report it to the Feds. because they're concerned about, guess what, drug money and, of course, terrorist money. I think the most you can deposit at any one time is about ten grand.

“Well, we’ve each got our separate accounts at two different banks, that should help, but, what are we going to do with the rest of it?“

“I guess we’ll have to leave it in a storage locker.”

“Well, that’s going to be a real hassle, when we return to Minnesota, carrying all that money with us everywhere we go.”

As Mike is looking over to Audrey while they are talking, he takes his eyes off the road for a second. When he returns his eyes to the road, suddenly there is a coyote chasing a rabbit across the road. He swerves to avoid hitting the coyote, and the CRV begins to skid on the loose rocks and gravel on the road and he loses control of the vehicle and they go off the road and plunge down a thirty foot embankment and hit a large boulder at the bottom. The airbags deploy as the CRV comes to an abrupt crashing stop.

“Are you okay?” Mike asks.

“Yeah, I think so. How about you?”

“I’m okay too,” He replies. The airbags saved us.”

“But, now what do we do?”

"Well, I guess we'll have to call a tow truck. Hopefully we are back in range of the Havasu cell towers."

He gets out his cell and calls triple 'A', which he has on speed dial and gives them their location. While they are waiting, they get out and survey the damage. The front end of the CRV is pretty well crunched. They check their backpack filled with the booty. It's fine and intact, just slammed around from the crash.

"I'm beginning to think that our backpack and its money are cursed," Mike says.

"What do we do with this now?" Audrey asks.

"Well, maybe we can ask the tow truck driver to drop us off at our condo. We'll have to stash the backpack there until we can get a new rental car and get it into a storage locker."

The tow truck arrives and pulls their CRV back up on the road and hooks it up and they both get into the truck. Audrey struggles to get up into the large truck with her sprained ankle. They explain to the driver that they want to stop by their condo and drop off their 'camping' gear so Audrey can start getting it cleaned up. The driver waits for them to run the backpacks into the condo. Audrey hobbles up the stairs where she stays behind and Mike goes with the tow truck to the Havasu Body Shop and checks their vehicle in and fills out the necessary insurance forms. He checks out a Hertz rental car and heads back to the condo.

Our snowbirds load the 'cursed' backpack into the rental car and head out in search of a rental storage locker.

They find a suitable locker, a fairly large one, stash the backpack and head to Wal-Mart where they purchase several folding tables.. When they return to the storage locker they open the backpack and spread out as much of the soggy money as they can, onto the tables to dry.

"Aren't we going to count it now, as we spread it out?"

"Nah, we can wait until it's dry and count it as we re-bundle it. We won't be able to deposit any of this until it's been dried out," Mike says.

"This could take a while," Audrey says, "There's no air movement in here."

So they head back to Wal-Mart and purchase a couple of fans.

"There, that should speed up the drying process," Mike says, as they set up the fans "We've got to get as much of this money as we can, into our bank accounts as soon as possible."

"So, now we wait," Audrey concludes.

* * * * * *

Days go by, then weeks. About every day or two, they go to the locker and re-bundle the dried bills and put out new bills to dry.

"This process is going quite well," Audrey says, "How much money do you think we're getting dried?"

"Well, you've gotta figure we can lay out about one hundred forty bills on each of the tables, times two; is two hundred eighty bills per run. Most of the bills are twenties, so times twenty equals five thousand, six hundred dollars per run. So far we've dried fourteen runs, for a grand total of seventy eight thousand dollars."

"Okay," Audrey says, "Maybe we should make a run to the banks with it. We can put twenty thousand in our two banks right here in Lake Havasu City. Then the rest of it we can run up to Vegas with, and open up some new bank accounts at several banks there. They have way more banks than here in Havasu. Besides, it's almost February fourteenth and remember, every year we go up to Vegas for a couple days of fun on Valentine's Day."

"That sounds like a great plan to me. Let's get started. First, I want to take the time to count all of the money and see just how much we have in this 'backpack from hell'.

The two snowbirds began counting their booty. They find one thousand, four hundred eighty two bundles of mostly twenties, but also a lot of bundles of one hundreds. That adds up to four million, four hundred eighty two thousand.

"That's plus the seventy eight thousand already dried. So, that's a grand total of four million, five hundred fifty six thousand dollars."

"Oh, my God," Audrey exclaims, "My knees go weak just thinking about that much money.

"Yeah, mine too. Those drug dealers must have sold a mountain of drugs to get this much money and it's all ours if we can process it carefully. That's an incredible amount of money to have sitting around. We've got to get it into bank accounts as quickly as possible. It looks like most of the rest of the money in thc bottom three-fourths of the backpack is dry. It's just the top money that got soaked from the rain."

"So, yeah," Audrey says, "We should be almost done with this drying phase."

"Yeah, let's gather up everything and head for Las Vegas they have a lot more banks there, than here in Havasu."

So when all the bills are dried, they bundle up the last batch of them and cram all of the bundles back into the backpack. Mike counts out ten thousand for each of their current bank accounts.

They lock up and leave for the day and head for their banks in Havasu to make those deposits. Later that evening, after dark, they return and load the backpack into their rented car and head out for Vegas.

SUSPICIONS AND SUSPECTS

Tucked in under a large cliff area alongside Highway 95 about ten miles south of Lake Havasu City, between the highway and the Colorado River just a short ways below the Parker Dam is the tiny office of the Buckskin Mountain State Park. There are only about a half dozen park rangers that work out of this office. The park itself is very small, encompassing a relatively small area that is bordered along highway 95 on the West and forms a triangle with the Bill Williams River on the North and a border that runs a diagonal jagged line from about a mile up the river, through the Buckskin Mountains back to the highway. They also manage a pair of bird sanctuary islands in the bottom end of Lake Havasu near the Parker Dam. The main job of the Park Rangers is to manage the bird populations on these lake islands and along Bill

Williams River. Their clientele are mainly bird watchers and backpackers who hike some of the more rugged mountain trails in the Buckskins.

The morning of February Fourteenth, Ranger Edward Diggeles arrives late to work. As he walks into the Rangers office, he finds all of the other rangers in a meeting. They are greeted by someone who introduces himself as Roger Morgan, Special Agent with the DEA, (Drug Enforcement Administration).

"My agency is investigating a very large shipment of drugs that has gone missing. Our informants in Mexico have been tracking this huge shipment of drugs that came up from Columbia last December. This shipment was supposed to have been flown across the border into Western Arizona, California, or Nevada. We tracked the flight by radar as it came across the border on Christmas Eve, but lost track of it as it flew into a large thunder storm near Quartzite and Parker. We think it may have been headed to Lake Havasu City or further north, up to the Laughlin or Las Vegas area. The plane never returned back into Mexico, so it may have run into some kind of mechanical trouble and was forced to land somewhere in the Tri-State area, or it crashed somewhere in that thunderstorm."

"Well," Ranger Diggeles says, "Has the plane been spotted on a landing strip, somewhere, or at any larger air field where they have mechanical facilities available?"

"We're still in the process of checking out all of those possibilities. We've also had search planes covering the entire area for the last month and a half, looking for a crash site, but you have to realize that this a huge area, covering hundreds of square miles. So far, we've found nothing. So, now we're checking with all public land based organizations, and asking them to keep on the lookout for any sign of a grounded plane or a crash site. Your area has a lot of very rugged terrain, here in the Buckskin Mountains with its jagged mountain peaks and deep canyons covered with thick foliage."

"Also, keep on the lookout for anyone exhibiting suspicious behavior, like they're searching for something. We have reason to believe that the drug cartel in Mexico that was responsible for the drug shipment also has their own agents here in the U.S. searching for that plane, same as we are. That shipment represents a huge loss for them. Our intel says probably several million dollars worth of cocaine."

The Park Supervisor, Steve Johnson stands up and speaks. "Why would the cartel be flying in the drug shipment? Everybody knows that the Colorado River is a super highway of drugs. They come across the border at San Luis and they run them up the river at night using their high speed boats. They have these thirty foot cats with a thousand horsepower engine that can travel ninety miles an hour."

"I know, their boats can outrun our boats. We tried to chase one of them last summer, so we followed it all the way up to Topock. We were so far behind that when we caught up to it, they had already dropped off all their drugs, so we had nothing. We've chased them sometimes all the way up to Laughlin, but with the same results."

"We've petitioned the Fed for money, but they said that those cats cost about a half million dollars, or more and there's no budget for it now we were told. Trump is sucking our budget dry for his "famous wall". His wall may keep out the illegal immigrants, but it's not doing squat for the drug traffic. These cartels are so rich, they just find another way. That plane load, I think, was an exception. I think the cartel had a rush order they wanted delivered, mostly to Las Vegas for the holidays. That place will go through a ton of drugs during the holidays."

Agent Morgan hands out his cards and asks them to call him with any sightings of the downed aircraft or of any suspicious behavior. With that, he leaves and the park Head Ranger, gets up again to speak to his crew.

"Okay people, here's the take on agent Morgan's talk this morning: we're not to do any kind of pursuing of anything or anyone suspicious. That's the DEA's job. We've got enough work to do this spring. We're short staffed after the budget cuts, and we still have to do repairs to the bird nesting areas on the Bill William River after the heavy winter rains and flooding. But, if you see, or hear anything suspicious, report it to Agent Morgan's office. You all have his card."

With that, the meeting is adjourned and everyone heads out to their jobsites for the day.

* * * * * *

Park Ranger Diggeles is troubled as he takes a two man crew up the Bill Williams River. They begin to work in the swampy area along the river, clearing away some of the flood debris from a nesting area of the Seagulls and Terns. As the crew is working, they are also discussing the morning's meeting with the DEA agent.

"Boy, oh boy," Ranger Leroy says, "Can you just imagine finding several million dollars' worth of drugs. I think if I found that drug plane with all those drugs on it, I'd be mighty tempted to just sell some of it before turning it in to that DEA agent. Boy, what I couldn't do with a million bucks."

"Now Leroy," Ranger Mike says, "I can't believe I just heard you say that. You couldn't just take some of the drugs and sell them. You're a sworn agent of the state of Arizona Park Service. That would be highly unethical and probably illegal. That would be tampering with evidence. You could go to jail for something like that."

"All right, all right, you two, just stop with that talk already." Ranger Diggeles says. "Why don't we take a lunch break now. I need to talk to you guys about something."

They find a raised rocky area at the edge of the swamp. After removing their waders, they open their lunch boxes and begin eating. A large

Bald Eagle flies overhead and lights in a tall mesquite tree as he makes his rounds up and down the river, in his quest for fish in the water and rodents in the tall marsh grass that borders the Bill Williams from Lake Havasu all the way to Alamo Lake.

As they are eating, Edward says, "Speaking of drugs, I have to tell you guys something that's been bothering me lately, especially after that meeting with that DEA agent. About two weeks ago, I was patrolling that area at the Eastern edge of the park where the river road ends and the trail begins. In that little parking area there, I came across an SUV parked there with the tail gate open and inside there were two people asleep. I thought I'd better see if they were alright. I looked into the back of the SUV as I went over to check on them. They had this huge backpack in there along with a smaller one. I woke them up and asked them the usual questions as I checked their IDs.

"They were a couple of snowbirds from Minnesota. Very nice folks. I told them they couldn't park there and sleep. It was against park rules. When I asked them about the huge backpack, they said, it was camping gear, that they had been up to Alamo Lake, camping. I said, "Okay," and we talked some more. I asked them about firearms, Blah, Blah, Blah. Then I told them everything was all okay and they should get some more rest before heading back to Lake Havasu. I wrote down their information and wished them a good day and left."

"But, now, I've been re-thinking that incident; especially after the meeting this morning with that DEA agent. I should have checked inside that backpack, shouldn't I? What do you guys think?"

"Well," Leroy says, "Heck yah. I would'a. But it's too late now. They're obviously long gone with the drugs by now."

"I think you better get on the phone with that DEA agent, right away, today," Mike says, "Somethings not right about that Minnesota couple's story about camping up at Alamo Lake. I've been up there camping before. You don't hike in all the way up the river trail to the campground and back. You would drive right into the camping area off of highway 93. to the East of Alamo Lake."

"I'd be willing to bet," says Leroy, "That they found the downed drug plane somewhere around Alamo Lake and they are transporting the drugs out, down the Bill Williams trail. It's safer than going out the main road through the campground. That's why the huge backpack. I'll bet that couple, aren't snowbirds from Minnesota at all. I'll bet they were drug cartel people with false ID's."

"You can't beat yourself up over it, Edward," Mike says, "At the time, there was no missing drug plane that you knew about. You can't just go digging through someone's backpack in the rear of their car without due cause. But you better have a talk with that DEA agent, first chance you get and let them take it from here."

Edward and his crew went back to work, cleaning up along the river. At quitting time, he dismissed them and they headed for home. Edward got on his cell phone and called the DEA Agent and told him about the incident of two weeks ago and he gave him the people's description, and the vehicle's description and the Minnesota license number.

"Well, it does sound suspicious enough to warrant some follow up by us. I wish you'd have called us earlier, but of course, no one knew about the plane yet at that time. I just hope the trail of those two hasn't gone too cold, but we'll get on it. We follow up on every lead we can get."

VIVA LAS VEGAS

"Happy Valentine's Day, Sweetheart," Mike says, from his side of the king bed, of their luxury suite at the MGM Grand hotel, "Is this how rich people live?"

"Happy Valentine's day to you also," Audrey says. You know, I think I could get used to this being rich," she says as she heads for the shower.

"Well, I don't think we're quite there yet, Honey. We've got to get our millions secured safely away," he says as he calls room service to order breakfast. "Although we've stashed our booty of cash in a safety deposit box at the City Bank when we first came into town, we can't just leave it sitting there. We've got to spread it around for safer keeping.

After their showers and breakfast, the new millionaire couple, get on their phones and begin looking for banks to deposit their newly begotten booty.

The snowbird millionaire couple spent about an hour looking up the nearest large banks, they came up with a list: Bank of America, Chase Bank, State Bank of Nevada, Citi Bank, and First State Bank of Las Vegas. But, after thinking about it and talking about it, they realize that at the rate of ten thousand dollar deposits into seven different banks, it would take about two hundred, fifty six deposits, and about thirty six months to accomplish it.

"We don't have that kind of time," Audrey says.

"I, know, I know. I'm thinking. How about this, we open up a business here in Las Vegas. I think the banks will allow a much bigger deposit from a business."

"That's a great idea, Mike. Why don't you check out how to register a new business here in Las Vegas? I think I'll go down to the casino and do some gambling to relieve some of the stress."

After about four hours, Audrey returns to their room, all excited.

Mike excitedly remarks, "I've just about got the set-up work done for our company. It's going to be a research company doing research on water usage here in Las Vegas, but it will take about a week to get it registered."

"Okay, that's great. Mike, but I think I've run across a quicker solution. I've been talking to the teller at the High Stakes Window - - - -.

"Wait, wait, wait, Audrey, you've been doing high-stakes gambling? We don't have our money secured yet."

"I know, I know, Mike, just hear me out. According to this teller, a lot of the high-stakes, high-rollers have their money in off-shore accounts. He says it's untraceable, and there's no taxes on the interest. He gave me the name of a local banker who can set us up with an account in The Cayman Islands."

"Oh, wow, that's great, Honey, you're a genius. I love you. I think though, I'll finish setting up the shell company though, just in case we need it in the future , and we can deposit a good chunk of the money into an account in the company's name for safe keeping for future use."

Mike finishes the application process for their research company. He finds an online web site and creates I.D.'s for both of them identifying them as owners of the new company; "Vegas Research Enterprise". Also on this web site he creates Nevada driver licenses for them. He grabs the laptop and an empty large brief case and they take off for the City Bank on the Vegas Strip in the uptown area. They extract a half million from their safety deposit box and load it into the large brief case. From there, they head over to the nearest US Bank where they sit down with a new-account specialist and present their new company ID's and ask to open a new account for their new company. Because they already have an account there, not too many questions are asked as they fill out an application for their new company and apply for a credit card, a cash card and an American Express Card account. When it's time to do the first deposit, some questions are asked about all the cash. Mike explains that the nature of their business is a cash only customer base. The New Account Specialist counts out the cash; five hundred thousand dollars, and makes the deposit. Mike takes the receipt and the other paperwork and puts it all into the brief case and they leave the bank.

"Okay," Mike says, "Let's go talk to this Cayman Island banker."

"But, let's not take any of the cash with us on this first trip," Audrey says, "Let's get some more information on this set-up. I don't know anything about these 'off-shore' banking places."

They find the bank; Las Vegas Savings and Loans, a small one story building just off Fremont Street, on Maryland Avenue, in "old Vegas". They go in and ask to see Frank, the name Audrey got from the casino teller. Mike introduces Audrey and himself and says he was referred by one of the tellers at the MGM casino.

"What can I do for you folks today?"

"We would like to see about opening up an account in the Cayman Islands."

"Okay, I'll need to see some identification and then we can begin the process."

They show him their drivers licenses.

"So you are from Minnesota? What brings you to Las Vegas?"

"Well, we are on business," Mike states, "We just recently opened up a new business here in Vegas and need somewhere to put our business profits."

"Okay, let's get started. Where are you staying here in Vegas?"

"We don't yet have a permanent residence. We're staying at the MGM."

"What's your room number? I'll need it for the account application."

"It's room number 1257."

He continues to enter the information into a computer. "And will you be transferring money from another bank, or do you have a bank cashier's check?"

"Well - - ah - - neither actually. We have a very large sum of money in cash."

"That's fine, we can accommodate that too. Do you have it with you?"

"No, we'll have to go and pick it up. Actually, we first wanted to find out just how it works to have an account in a foreign bank'"

"Well, it works just like an American bank, actually. Once the account is opened, you can deposit and withdraw from it just like any other bank. Well, it looks like the application is complete. Just sign here and I will get you an account number."

They both sign the application and Frank goes back to his computer and submits it to the Cayman Bank and Trust in the Cayman Islands. In a few minutes he gives them their new account number.

"Okay, then, Audrey, do you think that's straight forward enough?"

"Why, yes I do, Honey, why don't we go and get the cash right after lunch."

"Okay then," Mike says to the banker," We'll be back after lunch."

The snowbirds find a nice lunch place at a place called Schlotzsky's, just off the strip on Flamingo Road. They order Schlotsky's famous roast beef sandwiches and cokes and began discussing their new situation.

* * * * *

At 267 Washington Avenue in downtown Las Vegas on the eighth floor of the Federal Building, in the office of the regional DEA, Special Agent Roger Morgan is on the phone with one of his agents in the field. Agent Joe Thompson is calling from Lake Havasu City, Arizona.

"Roger, I have just completed the investigation of the possible connection between that missing plane load of cocaine and the couple from Minnesota. I have reason to believe that they are somehow involved in it. I haven't found proof yet because I haven't yet caught up with them. I traced their car license plates that we got from that park ranger to an insurance claim filed recently. The car is in a body shop here in Havasu with some major front end damage. They probably went off the road on that rugged trail along the Bill Williams River. I got the information on their rental car. However, they are not in town. I checked their condo and they haven't been there in a while and there is no sign of any of the drugs. But I came across the phone number of a friend of theirs; a Bill and Mia Wilson. I called them to see if they had any knowledge. They are both residents here in Havasu and have been tied up with fulltime work. However Mia stated that the Minnesotans typically go to Vegas for Valentine's Day. So far, that's all I have. It's my opinion that they will be trying to sell the coke in Vegas. We all know how easy it is to sell drugs in Vegas. I'll give you their rental car info. It looks like the ball is in your court up there in Vegas."

"Okay Joe, thanks for the update. We'll take over here in Vegas. We'll let you know if they head back to Havasu. Meantime, I'll turn our case over to the FBI. Because they have crossed state lines in the commission of a crime, it now becomes a federal case."

* * * * *

Across town, in downtown Las Vegas, in another office high rise, ninth floor, a meeting was under way.

The office was not well defined or advertised. The name on the door merely had a logo with a green, white and red panel, the colors of the Mexican flag. The middle white section contained the name in a circular pattern; Medellin Transfer Company – SW Division. This was the district office of the Medellin Drug Cartel. It was headquartered in Las Vegas because Las Vegas was the biggest market in the southwest US. Bigger even than LA.

Rickardo Mendosa slammed his hand down hard on the conference table. He was the Southwest district director.

"I want answers," he yelled at the other eight men seated around the table, "I want answers now."

They were the local agents from the major cities on the west coast and also Salt Lake City and Phoenix and, of course, Las Vegas.

"Dammit, I want to know what the hell happened to that shipment that we lost last Christmas Eve. You have had enough time to investigate its disappearance. I am under extreme pressure from our home office in Bogota. They are screaming at me to find that shipment. It had a net dollar amount of almost ten million US dollars. The people in Bogota are not going to give up until they have answers. That means neither can we. This is now our top priority. We've got to find that shipment. I want all of you to work your districts. See if there are any clues where that plane load of coke could have disappeared to. Francesco, you work for the DEA. What are they doing to locate that plane?"

"Well sir, the latest info that I have; is that they are following up on a lead that the plane went down somewhere in the Mojave near Alamo Lake in Arizona, and they have reason to believe some of the lost shipment is being transported up here to Vegas by unknown persons. But they don't have details yet and they don't know just where the plane is. Also, the Central US district office in St. Louis has called and said their portion of the shipment didn't get there and their two transporters are missing, along with their plane."

"What the hell is going out there?" Rickardo yelled at them again. "Manuel, you have the Phoenix district. You have direct ties to the distribution center in Chihuahua. Get on the phone and find out if that shipment actually went out. Follow up with everyone connected with the transporter who picked up the shipment. Pressure these people for answers. Come on people, get off your fat asses and get answers. Bogota wants answers, dammit, I want answers."

* * * * *

There was a knock on the door of the Ramirez family house on Avenue De Leones in Chihuahua, Mexico. It is now mid-May, almost five months from that fateful Christmas Eve on that high plateau in the Buckskin Mountains of Arizona. It is late afternoon. The children are all home from school, the Mendoza children; Juanita, Madeline, Juan and Antonio, as well as the two Ramirez children; Joseppi and Christina. They are not alarmed by someone knocking at the door. There had been all kinds of people coming to the house since the Mendoza kids moved in. First there was the welfare people, making sure the children were getting settled in and well cared for. Then the school representative, getting them registered in the new school. The priest from the local Catholic Church stopped by to welcome them into the new parish. Last March, someone from the drug cartel came by to ask the Mendoza's questions about their parent's departure on that terrible Christmas Eve.

"Could you please answer the door," their mother, Carlotta yelled to her husband, Antonio, who had just arrived home a few minutes before, "I'm quite busy getting dinner prepared."

The man at the door introduced himself as agent Juan Carlos, agent with the Mexico Federales Investigation Department. He showed Antonio his ID and said he had some news about the Mendoza's. Antonio invited him to come in. He was not an agent with the Mexico Federales, however. He was from the Medellin drug cartel, sent to their house to question the Mendoza's and the whole family and to extract what information he could about the missing drug shipment. He couldn't care less about Xavier and Maria. While he did have some news to share, he was mainly there to question the children again, about their parent's whereabouts.

They all gathered and were seated in the living room. Juan began by saying how sorry he was that no news was yet available about the exact whereabouts of the children's parents.

"We are following up on several leads about what may have happened to them in the USA. We believe that they may possibly be in Las Vegas. We know that your mother has a sister who lives in Las Vegas. We will be questioning her shortly to see if your mother has made recent contact with her. We have retrieved the cache of letters between your mother and her sister from your old home in La Junta when we searched the house. We therefore, know that your parents and you kids were conspiring with your aunt to escape from Mexico and join her in Las Vegas. Now, I need to know if you kids have heard anything from your parents or your aunt in Las Vegas?"

"We have heard nothing from anyone about this conspiracy to go to USA," Antonio declared emphatically.

Juan, like most cartel members, operated on a very short fuse. He leaped to his feet and confronted Antonio.

"You just shut the hell up," he yelled at Antonio, "I wasn't talking to you. I was asking the kids."

With that he pulled out a gun and stuck it in Antonio's face, then started waving it around. "I am not screwing around with you," He yelled, as he shot a hole in the ceiling, "I want answers, dammit, and I want them now."

With that, he went over to where Juanita was sitting and grabbed her by the hair and pulled her up out of her chair and put the gun to her head.

"Now, I'll ask one more time, have any of you heard from your parents?"

"No, sir, we haven't," they all answered together in trembling voices.

"Well, I think you're a bunch of lying little bastards," he said, as he took his gun and cracked Juanita across the side of her face. "If I find out you're lying to me, I'll rape you right here in front of your whole family."

She began sobbing as she held the side of her face and blood began trickling down.

"You just leave her alone," Antonio yelled at him, "She knows nothing."

Juan then turned and faced Antonio. "I thought I told you to shut the hell up."

With that, he raised his gun and shot Antonio in the head and he crumpled to the floor as his wife Carlotta screamed and ran to him, dead on the floor and began sobbing uncontrollably. The children all began crying loudly as they ran to their mother and their dead father. Juan grabbed Juanita, by her hair again and forced her into her bedroom and shoved her down on the bed. She began sobbing loudly and begging, "No, no, no, please, no."

He knew he would not dare to touch her. He had strict orders not to harm any of the Mendoza children until they heard from their parents.

"Shut the hell up," Juan yelled at her, "I'm not going to hurt you yet. As long as you stay put while I search your room. If I find anything from your parents or your aunt in Las Vegas, then I'll rape you right here in your own bed."

With that, he began to tear apart her bedroom. He did not find anything recently linking her to her parents or to her aunt in Las Vegas. He went over to the bed and began beating Juanita some more with his pistol and fists until her head and upper body were bloody and raw and she was barely conscious. Then he proceeded to rape her.

"Well, it looks like you will live, for now anyway," He said afterward, "If you hear from any of them, your parents, or that aunt in Las Vegas you'd better call me, or another family member will die."

With that, he took out one of his calling cards and dropped it on top of her bloodied body and turned and left her there, lying on the bed, sobbing uncontrollably and barely conscience. He walked out of the bedroom and right past the man he had just murdered along with the sobbing family without even looking at any of them. As he left the house though, he began processing what had just happened. He knew that when he reported back into the cartel headquarters, that he did not extract the information they had sent him to gather, the same fate awaited him. Such was the nature of the Medellin cartel.

Back at the house, Juanita lay on her bed still sobbing uncontrollably from the terror and the beating and rape she had just experienced from the cartel thug who had just raped her and murdered her foster father. But after a while, as she gained control of her sobbing, she began thinking and processing a course of action for her and her family. She would have the last laugh against the thug that beat and raped her and the cartel that sent him. Little did they know that before the cartel had searched her old house, just before she and her siblings left for their new foster home, she had discovered the lock-box that her parents had been putting their savings into. There was almost twenty thousand U.S. dollars in the lock-box. She had put it into her jewelry chest and brought it with to their new home and hid it in her little sister's bedroom instead of her own bedroom.

She now knew that there was only one course of action to take in order to survive. She and the rest of her family, including her foster family would use the money to escape to America. She felt with certainty that before this was over, they would all be murdered by the cartel just like her foster dad, if they didn't make a run for it.

After the funeral for Antonio, after all the guest mourners had left, Juanita gathered all the children and their foster mom, Carlotta around the kitchen table. They couldn't bear to get together again in the living room. No one wanted to ever go in there again after what happened in there to their father. Juanita told them in a whisper about the money and her plan to use it to escape to America. She gave all the children a warning that they were not to tell anyone else of their plan or they would all end up dead, just like their father. Their mom, Carlotta, said she would contact the Mendoza's aunt in Las Vegas and tell her of their plan and see if she could help. Juanita gave Carlotta the phone number and name; Lucita Adriana, of their aunt in Las Vegas

Next day, after the children all left for school - -, with another stern warning about their secret plan and a warning that they were probably being watched by cartel people, Carlotta picked up her shopping bags and left for the market. She left the youngest two with a neighbor. After shopping for a number of food items, she had the shopping bags nearly full. Before leaving for home, she looked carefully around to make sure she wasn't being followed. She stepped cautiously off the main market street into a private little alcove that had a pay phone. She deposited several pesos into the phone slot and dialed the number that Juanita had given her.

"Is this Lucita Adriana?" she questioned.

"Why, yes it is, and who is this calling?" came the reply.

"Are you alone?" Carlotta first asked.

"Well, almost. My husband Joseppi was just leaving for work. Who is this calling please?"

"Let me explain. I'm sorry for all the questions but I am in a desperate situation. My name is Carlotta Ramirez. I am foster mom to the Mendoza children. I don't know if you've heard that they have been orphaned and living with Antonio and me because of the disappearance of their parents."

"Oh, my God! I've been wondering why I haven't heard from Maria since before Christmas. What happened to Maria and Xavier?"

"Nobody knows. They just disappeared on one of their drug runs last Christmas. The authorities think that their plane crashed somewhere in the US, although they haven't found any wreckage of it. But, the Medellin drug cartel thinks they may be alive still. They want their drug money, of course. They sent one of their thugs to our house about three days ago and started to question the children if they had heard from their parents. They haven't, of course. But then things got really awful." she said, as she began sobbing into the phone. He, - - - He - - , shot my husband, Lucita, - - - this devil, - - -he just shot Antonio in the head,- - - right in front of the children, - - -, after Antonio defended the children and insisted that no one has heard from Maria and Xavier. - - - - Then he dragged Juanita into her bedroom and said he was going to rape her if he found any proof that she had been in contact with her parents. He tore her room apart, but didn't find anything, of course. Then he raped her anyway and threatened her again and said that she had better let him know if anyone hears from Maria and Xavier, or he would be back and rape her again and kill another one of the family. I'm telling you, this man is the devil and that drug cartel is evil, evil, evil. They are all right out of hell. They will kill us all, Lucita. I feel I must warn you, they will come for you too."

"Oh, Carlotta, I'm so, so sorry for what you have been through. You know, I told Maria many times. I warned her about what they were doing, running drugs for the cartel. But she insisted that it was just temporary and that they were making a lot of money and soon they would have enough to move their family here to the US. I tried to tell her that she and Xavier were just dancing with the devil, doing business with the cartel. I said that one day the devil would want his due, and that he would come for their souls. And it looks like the devil has done just that. He's coming for his due Carlotta, and we are all going to have to pay."

"But, can you help us Lucita? We have to get out of Mexico. They are going to kill us all, I just know it. And, I must warn you Lucita, they will come for you too. This evil cartel already owns Mexico. They are more powerful than our police and maybe even our government. They have their evil tentacles reaching into the US as well. I think that we must all just disappear. I was hoping you could help us to get out of Mexico. We have some money. Juanita found a very large sum of money at their old house before they came to live with us that Xavier and Maria had stashed away."

"I, too have some escape money. Maria and Xavier had been sending me some money regularly to keep safe for them when they decided to come here to Las Vegas to live. I opened up a special bank account for them. I agree with you, Carlotta, we need to disappear or get killed by those evil bastards from the cartel. Fortunately, Maria and I had devised a plan to use in case they needed to get out of Mexico. We can use that plan to get your family out now. First, we had false Id's made up for Maria and Xavier and the kids, as well as Joseppi and myself. I will get one's made up for you and your children. If you can give me the name and address of a friend of yours that you can trust, I will mail them to you. Call me when you get them. I will give you instructions how to proceed to get across the border at El Paso, where we will meet you."

"God bless you Lucita, maybe this will be our salvation from this hell that has been cast upon us."

With that they both hung up and Carlotta picked up her shopping bags and carefully looked around. No one was watching or following her as she made her way back home. That evening at dinner, she explained to the children what she had set up as a plan with Lucita so far. She told the children that as soon as they received the information in the mail, they would be leaving their home and school for good to keep from being killed like their father was. She warned them that their lives depended on them not telling anyone they would be leaving. Later that evening, she called her friend, Angelina and asked if it was ok to have some mail delivered to her address.

About a week later, Carlotta's friend from across town, Angelina, knocked on the door. She handed her an envelope.

"I won't ask what is in the envelope," she said, "I am your life-long friend and I will respect your privacy. But, if there's anything else I can do, please let me know. I heard about your husband Antonio and I am so very sorry. I'll just say that I've seen this sort of thing happen before. Let me help you Carlotta. I've helped other families before. Please, let me help you get your family to El Paso. I know how to get you there with what's in the envelope. Carlotta, it's happening all over Mexico. People are fleeing this country that we once loved. We are being driven out by the drug cartels. They are killing and torturing us every day over their drug business. Our government can't even help us. The cartels own our officials. Now, even the big and powerful country of the US is turning its back on us. That new president, Senior Trump is blaming us for trying to escape from a deathly condition here, that his government has failed to come to terms with. If there were no addicts in the US, there would be no drug trafficking from Mexico. Hence, no drug cartels and no immigration problem. We are the victims here, of a failed program in the US to fix their own drug addiction problems. Trump and his congress want to spend billions on a wall to keep us out. But he is an idiot to not see that his wall will not solve the drug problem. Cannot they see that there is an immigration problem because there is an uncontrolled addiction problem in the US. Those billions should be spent to fix the US addiction problem. Then there would be no need for a wall."

"I'm sorry, Carlotta. It seems like I'm ranting about something neither one of us can fix."

"It's alright Angelina, I'm starting to get a better idea of the bigger picture. I would be so appreciative of you helping us get to El Paso. I'll call you as soon as we are ready to go."

"Okay, but don't wait too long. I have to make reservations for us on the bus to Juarez."

"Oh, are you coming with us?"

"Yes, I'll come with as far as Juarez. My husband and I both work at the DELCO plant there. I'll show you where to catch the bus that takes workers from the DELCO battery plant in Juarez across the river border to El Paso."

As Angelina leaves, Carlotta opens the envelope.

LEAVING LAS VEGAS

WITH MONEY

Mike and Audrey began discussing their options while they enjoyed their Schlotzsky's sandwiches.

"Do we still want to put the rest of our money into this "offshore" account?" Audrey asks, "Or, should we just wait and see if we can find some other place to invest it?

"Well, honestly, I just don't trust this banker. He seemed awfully anxious to just get ahold of our money. How about we split up what's left of the money, put half into the offshore account and the other half into a stock market investment account?"

"Okay, let's go back to our hotel room and pick up a couple more brief cases, then go to our safety deposit box and get another half mil. to put in the offshore account."

When they got back to their hotel room, however, they noticed something out of place. In fact a lot is out of place, the room had been gone through, or “tossed”, as they say, or searched.

“What the hell is going on here?” Mike asked, ”Was it just some random burglary or has somebody found out about the money and thought that maybe we kept it here in the hotel room?”

“I don’t know, but we had better just get out of here.”

They packed up everything and quickly checked out of the MGM Grand hotel, but as they are about to get to their car, they saw somebody breaking into it. Quickly, they got out of the ramp without being seen, and ran to the front door of the hotel and hailed a cab. Mike told the driver to take them to the Venetian Hotel. When they got to their new room, they collapsed onto the bed.

“What the heck is going on?” Audrey asks, rhetorically.

“Okay, I sure as heck don’t know, but I think that we should now just put all the rest of the money into that offshore account and get the heck out of this town. I think someone is after us. Could be the FBI. Could be the DEA. Could be the drug cartel. Could even be that banker. He’s the only one that we gave our hotel room number to."

"Well, let's get over to our safe deposit box and get the rest of the money out before the box can be traced."

With that said, they take their two large duffle bags and get over to Citi Bank and empty out their safe deposit box and head over to the offshore banker. But first, they stop at a Fidelity investment office and deposit two of the millions into their already established investment account. Mike showed them his business ID and explained again that the business is run on cash transactions. In Vegas, banks and investment companies don't ask too many questions. They just assume the money is either casino winnings or drug money.

While the investment broker was counting their money, Mike said "After we get all of this money taken care of; we have to get to a Post Office and submit a 'change-of-address' form to have our mail forwarded back to our home in Minnesota and held at the Post Office there. We'll designate one of the kids to pick it up periodically and hold on to it until we get back. We can't trust it going to our condo in Havasu anymore. Whoever is following us and broke into our hotel room at the MGM will surely be watching our mail in Havasu."

"Yes, I agree, We don't know if it was FBI, DEA, or a drug cartel, but we probably can't go back to our condo again to stay, but we should slip back there and get all of our stuff and get checked out."

When they got to the Las Vegas Savings and Loans bank, they first asked the receptionist if Frank was back from lunch yet.

"Oh, Frank didn't go out to lunch today. He just ate a sandwich and a coffee at his desk."

That was a relief to them both. At least they now knew that it wasn't Frank who broke into their hotel room, looking for their money. Frank came out to greet them and they went back to his office where Frank took their many bundles of bills and ran them through a counting machine. Mike, however decided to keep out fifty thousand dollars, 'just in case" he told Audrey. After Frank ran the cash downstairs to the vault, he came back with a receipt.

"You're all set,: He said, "The money will be available to you in ten business days."

Mike checked the receipt and handed it to Audrey for verification. It read, one million. nine hundred, fifty thousand dollars. They both thanked Frank and took a cab back to their new hotel, the Venetian.

“Well, we can’t stay here either,” Audrey says, “What are we going to do? Where are we going to go next?”

“We need to get us another car and not another rental. They can trace those too, obviously. We’ll need to buy one. But not here in Vegas, they can trace those too. I think we should head for LA. They can’t possibly trace all the cars in LA. We can take the bus.”

“Okay then, let’s just get going. It won’t take long to pack. We don’t have many clothes left. We left most of them in Havasu. Oh darn, guess we’ll have to do some clothes shopping in LA. But first, we should call our friends in Havasu and let them know that we had to leave Havasu early this year because of a family situation.”

Audrey called their friends in Havasu and they agreed to pack the rest of their stuff into storage and get them checked out of the condo. Meanwhile, Mike called the greyhound bus depot and asked what time they have a bus to LA after midnight. The ticket agent told him; two A.M. Audrey called room service for dinner, after which they set the alarm and tried to get some sleep. About one, A.M. they checked out and got a cab to the bus depot.

The snowbirds arrived in LA at six A.M. It’s rush hour in LA so they checked in to a “No-

Name" motel, one that probably wouldn't be traced by the FBI or the DEA and found a diner close by and had breakfast while they waited for rush hour to subside. Here they continued discussing their dilemma.

Okay, how's this for a plan," Mike suggests, "We get the car here in LA, then we hit the road up the coast to Oregon. We'll get a PO. Box in Portland so we can have our mail routed there."

"That's a good plan, Mike. How about we then get an apartment there, in Oregon, so we have a sort of home base until everything dies down and we can start living a normal life again."

"Okay, then, let's get the car license issued there in Oregon. That way it'll be harder to trace the car."

After breakfast, the rush hour subsided somewhat. It seems like it's always rush hour in LA. The two snowbirds headed out to find a car dealer. They're lucky, they ended up in a part of LA, that had a ton of car dealers. They are on Manchester Blvd. in the town of Inglewood. As they were walking along looking at the car dealers, they finally spot what looks like a reputable dealer.

"I've always wanted to drive a brand new car," Audrey declares.

"Even with our "measly" millions however, we can't buy new. We have to get something inconspicuous. So let's just ask to see a "previously owned" one."

As they approach a salesman, they asked to see a "previously owned" Chevy Impala. one of Chevy's luxury sport sedans. He found them a two year old, previously owned black one.

"Perfect," Audrey says, "It has really low miles, only thirty thousand miles, let's test drive it."

After the test drive, the salesperson says, "I think this was a rental car, that's why the low miles. It lists at twenty one thousand."

"We'll take it at eighteen." Mike says, as he handed him his American Express card. He gave him their address in Minnesota, as he explains that they flew out on vacation, but decided to stay and find a place to live in LA.

"Well, this is one of the finest road cars that Chevrolet makes," the dealer said as he wrote up the order and associated paper work for Mike to sign and told them the new license plates will be mailed to their address in Minnesota. Our two snowbirds jumped in and headed back to their sleazy motel and checked out.

Mike found the 405 freeway and they headed north out of LA and picked up the I-5, which would take them all the way north into Oregon.

THE ROAD LESS TRAVELED AND FOLLOWED

Rain, - - - it's what it does, in western Oregon in the spring, especially in the mountains, where it sometimes rains nonstop for days, and sometimes turns to snow. And, there are a lot of mountains in western Oregon.

Mike looked out their second floor motel window in Grants Pass, Oregon in the early morning, at the rain coming down.. It was still dark outside, especially with the rain. They had driven through the rain until late last night, but wanted to get an early start this morning, on their way to Portland. As he looked down below to where their car was parked, Mike saw two men next to their car. One was at the trunk, and was attempting to open it. The other one was at the passenger's side door and had already jimmied it open. Just as he was about to yell at them, the motel desk clerk came out of the office. His shift was over and he was headed home.

"Hey, what the hell is going on here," the motel clerk yells, "I'm going to call 911"

The two would-be burglars stopped what they were doing and scurried back to their car which was parked right behind Mike and Audrey's Impala and took off. As the motel clerk continued walking down the long front of the building to his car, he saw that the door to the room just below Mike and Audrey's was standing open, but the room was dark inside.

The clerk rushed back to the office and called Mike and Audrey's room on the second floor to let them know that their other room was also probably broken into. He doesn't know they are husband and wife. When they checked in the night before, they used their false ID's to get the separate rooms to avoid anyone following them. This break-in just confirmed their worst fears. Someone has indeed been following them, all the way from LA.

"But who?" Audrey asks Mike, "Would it be the DEA? Or maybe that evil drug cartel?"

"I don't have any idea either, but we better hurry and hit the road again."

The motel clerk informs Mike that he has to call the police. "It's motel policy, anytime there is a break-in. Is your business partner OK? She's not still in the room, is she?"

"No, she's up here, we were just about to head out for breakfast. Did you get a license plate number?"

"No, I couldn't see it from where I was standing."

"Well, I did. I could see it from up here," Mike says, as he writes it down on a motel note pad.

Mike told him that they are leaving and they both hang up. Mike and Audrey hurry and get packed up again. Not even time to shower or brush teeth. They hurried downstairs to their car and were just about to unlock it and get in, when the Clerk comes rushing out of the office.

"Wait - - , wait - -, wait, you can't get back in your car yet. Your car is now a crime scene"

About five minutes later a local squad car pulled up out front. The police checked the car over and dusted it for prints. The officer in charge asked them about the temporary permit sticker in the back window and asked to see their ID's and registration. Mike hit the open button on his key fob and told him to look in the glove box.

"So, you're snowbirds, taking the scenic route back to Minnesota? I'm afraid I'm going to have to, have a look in your suitcases." the officer says as his partner picks up the first bag and opens it on the trunk of the squad car and goes through it, and then the other one.

"Nothing in either of them." He reports.

"No, we're out here on business and headed to Portland. Our other car broke down in LA and we had to get a new one." Mike lied, "Here, I got the license plate number of their car."

He handed the officer the note with the number on it.

"Thanks," the officer said, "we'll get an APB out on it right away

"Were you in your motel room when they broke in there?" he asks Audrey, as they walk over to the still open door of the motel room.

"No, I had just packed up and went up to make sure Mike was up so we could hit the road

The two policemen check the room over and dust the door for prints.

"Boy, oh boy, they really trashed this room. Any idea what they might have been looking for? Did you have anything of value in here?"

"No," Audrey stated, "Just normal stuff, clothes and toiletries, which I had already packed up. We're not going to be liable for the damages in there, are we?"

"No, no, the motel clerk said, "we have insurance coverage for that."

"Probably just some 'dirt-bags' looking for drugs. Well, then, I guess you are free to go. I'll write up a report for the motel's insurance, as long as you two guests haven't had anything stolen."

Mike and Audrey picked up their bags and threw them in the back and climbed into their car, at last, to head out.

"O. M. G." Audrey exclaimed after they were gassed up and looking for a restaurant for breakfast.

"I was just thinking how bad that would have been if that would have happened in Vegas. We would be sitting in jail right now, trying to explain the four million dollars in our luggage."

"Yeah, I guess we were lucky. I guess life is just a matter of lucky or unlucky situations."

"Well, I think the Lord is looking out for us because we're basically good Christian people."

"Who just happened to run across a really lucky find of a couple million unlucky dollars."

"Oh, just stop with the lucky, unlucky talk. This money was truly a gift from God and I think we need to try and do some good with it. Are you a good Christion, or not?"

"Yeah, I think I am, and we should give a bunch of it to the church and charities."

"Well, okay, that's a better attitude."

They found a restaurant just before the on-ramp to I-5. During breakfast, they discussed their dilemma and their options.

"What if whoever broke into our motel room was FBI, or DEA," Audrey says, "If so, maybe they already have an APB out on us, instead of that other car."

"And what if it was that drug cartel? I think, whoever is on our tail, we need to stay off of the interstate here in Oregon. The US Highway Patrol has all the electronic tracking equipment, even helicopters."

Their suspicions were confirmed when four Highway Patrolmen came in and sat down in the next booth and began discussing all the current APBs that they had to follow up on for the day. Mike could have sworn that he heard their black Chevy Impala mentioned. They didn't even finish their breakfast. As soon as the waitress brought the tab, they got up and paid the tab and hurriedly left. They felt lucky the highway patrols were parked around the corner from them. Mike checked their map and picked a state highway number 199 that would take them south, back into California to the town of Crescent City. As they were leaving, Mike carefully checked for anyone following them.

They found a no-name motel in Crescent City and stayed put for three days. They didn't dare drive their car. They walked to restaurants and went for long hikes along the ocean shore. After three days there hadn't been anyone trying to break into their room or car and they were getting anxious to get on the road again. On the fourth day, they packed up their things and checked out of their motel again.

Mike said, "I think it will be safe now to head north again, across Oregon, but we've still gotta stay off of the freeways."

They left Crescent City and headed up highway 101, the coastal highway and back up into Oregon. Mike followed the 101 all the way up the coast to the town of Florence on the coast. Here they stopped for the night. They again checked their map.

"Looks like we could cut over toward Eugene and pick up a highway 99W which parallels Interstate 5 going north," Audrey stated.

"I agree," Mike replied, "We need to get off of this coastal highway. It's too slow going and looking north there will be a crowd of vacation people going to the beaches and that means a lot of cops. But I don't want to go anywhere near any large city. Let's take this lesser road, number 36 into Junction City north of Eugene and pick up highway 99W there. From there we can get on highway 47 which will take us all the way up into Washington. We'll cross the Columbia river at the town of Longview and get back on I-5."

"OK, looks like we'll hang out in Washington for a while until everything settles down."

* * * * * *

Lunchtime in the cafeteria on the third floor of the Federal Building in North Las Vegas, DEA Special Agent Roger Morgan and FBI District Director Rick Nelson are having lunch together. They began discussing the case of the planeload of missing drugs.

"Here's what we have so far," Agent Nelson reports. "The plane left Mexico from somewhere near the city of Chihuahua last Christmas Eve. Our border radar tracked it crossing into Arizona east of Yuma, heading due north. But our radar site in the town of Parker lost them in a thunder storm. I think we can safely assume they were headed north to a landing site somewhere near Las Vegas. That's the biggest market for drugs in the entire southwest. We have searched all up and down Lake Havasu and the entire Colorado River Valley, all the way up to Bullhead City, Boulder City and every possible landing site in and around Vegas. There has been absolutely no sign of that plane. It has simply disappeared, along with most of the drug shipment. Our sources here in Vegas have confirmed that a small shipment of the drugs did make their way into Vegas over the holidays. The only lead we have is from a park ranger at the Bill Williams State Park. He claims that he came across two people in his park area who he claims could have been from the Medellin Drug Cartel on a mission to retrieve their drugs from a supposed crash site near Alamo Lake. He claims that they had ID's of two snowbirds from Minnesota. This park ranger supposes that the two cartel people may have murdered the two snowbirds and stole their ID's. However, it appears the two supposed drug retrievers have vanished. After tracking them here to Vegas, we lost them and their trail has gone cold. But we really need more proof that they were involved in the missing drug plane before we can issue an arrest warrant."

"Well, here's what the FBI has, so far." Director, Rick Nelson begins, "We have a mole inside the cartel who reports to us regularly. He says that the cartel has followed the two from Las Vegas to Los Angeles where they supposedly bought a car and headed up the coast into Oregon. There was some kind of confrontation up there with the local police and two of the cartel agents and they lost track of them. However, Oregon has issued an APB on them in Oregon on suspicion of dealing drugs. We haven't heard back yet if they fled back into California, or made it up into Washington. We are in contact with the Oregon Highway Patrol, but so far, nothing."

* * * * * *

The bridge over the Columbia River appeared dimly lit at half-past midnight as a heavy fog crept up the river valley from the Pacific Ocean. Like a giant cloud that had sunk to the earth's surface. It began forming miles out from shore. Here, the frigid waters of the Pacific Oceanic Stream, chilled by glacial melt flowed south right out of the Gulf of Alaska. When these cold waters met the relative warm waters of the Columbia River flowing out to meet them, fog began forming and was swept inland, up the river valley. Like a giant living creature, this fog monster swallowed everything in its path. It swallowed first the city of Astoria near the coast and all the smaller towns and roadways. It swallowed the town of Longview, where they were headed, and by morning this fog monster would engulf the entire city of Portland before being melted away by the morning sun.

"This is really creepy," Audrey all but whispered to Mike as they began to cross the

Columbia River bridge from Oregon into Washington. "There could be anything, or anybody out there waiting for us on the other side of this bridge. Like maybe, the FBI, or those two agents from the drug cartel that almost got us, back at our motel in Grants Pass in Oregon, or maybe the Oregon Highway Patrol."

"I'll have to agree with you, Honey, It is creepy, and you can't see twenty feet in front of the car. But," He tried to reassure her, "There is no one out there waiting for us. No one knows we're coming across here into Washington. I firmly believe that we've ditched everyone that was following us."

But, little did they know, Mike couldn't have been more wrong - - - - -.

* * * * * *

In the town of Longview, a contingent of a squadron of law enforcement people had gathered outside the Sheriff's department comprised of agents from the FBI, DEA and the local Sheriff's Department's SWAT team.

"I can't believe that this is all the personnel that our departments could muster up for this operation," The lead FBI agent was heard complaining to the head DEA agent. "How are we supposed to run a successful sting operation with only about six people?"

"Well, I guess all we can do is set up a road block at the bridge. I sure hope our informant is right in saying that they will be arriving tonight in this fog. I don't know if this fog will work for us or against us."

"Well, let's get out to the bridge and see if they show up, and if we can see them in this fog."

Meanwhile, already at the mouth of the bridge, two of the cartel agents were already set up. They couldn't create a roadblock with just a single car, so they parked on the narrow shoulder at the edge of the steep embankment about twenty yards up from the bridge. The bridge and the embankment were about fifty feet above the river. When the FBI, DEA and local law enforcement arrived at the bridge they found that the fog was so thick that they couldn't see their hands in front of their faces and didn't see the cartel car parked along the edge of the highway.

After they set up their roadblock with two of their squad cars parked across the mouth of the bridge, the sheriff said, "This is not good, boys. This is one of the thickest fogs I've seen in quite some time. We can't see them coming, and they won't be able to see us until they are right on top of us. Can't we just tail them when they come through? We could then pull them over north of

Longview where the fog is a lot lighter. This is very dangerous."

"I know," the lead FBI agent replied, "But we have orders to carry out this sting tonight, here and now."

They then all took up positions on the back sides of the two blocking vehicles. They drew their guns and waited.

* * * * *

"You better slow down, Mike," Audrey said, "You can't possibly see even the front of your hood."

"I know, Honey," he replied as he slowed to about five miles-per-hour.

When they got to about the middle of the bridge, however, the fog appeared to lesson quite a bit, probably pushed away by the wind coming up the river valley. Mike again picked up speed, to about fifty.

"Be careful, Mike," Audrey warned, "There's more thick fog at the end of the bridge."

But Mike ignored the warning, saying, "I just want to get off this bridge. Maybe the fog lets up further down the road, once we get past this bridge."

With that, Mike slammed into the fog bank at the end of the bridge at about fifty miles per hour. In the thick, black fog, he didn't see the two squad cars blocking the bridge exit with their lights flashing. Nor did he see any of the law enforcement contingent who barely heard them coming through the thick, black fog and began firing at them before they could even see them.

"Look out!" was all that Audrey could scream, as they slammed into one of the squad cars, pushing it over the edge of the highway and through the ancient cable and post guard rail. The impact carried three members of the SWAT team with the squad car. The rotted cable posts snapped off. The cables broke loose from the bridge structure and the squad car went over the edge and dropped fifty feet onto the river bank below. The three SWAT members were crushed as the car landed on top of them. Meantime, the rest of the team continued to fire at Mike and Audreys car but not hitting the black car in the thick black fog. Their Chevy Impala spun around three hundred sixty degrees from the impact. Their airbags deployed as the Impala also slammed into the cable guard rail further down and snapped off several of the rotted posts. The cables became entangled in the crushed front end of the Impala and prevented it from plunging down the fifty foot embankment. Their Impala hung there, in mid-air, just over the edge of the embankment suspended by the cables.

"Oh, my God - -, Oh my God," Audrey screamed, as the airbags deflated. "Where are we?"

Neither of them could see anything in the blackness. Fortunately for them, they couldn't see that they were suspended fifty feet above the river shore, held up by the cables. As they slowly unfastened their seat belts, Audrey tried her door, but, of course it was crushed shut by the impact. They both crawled into the back seat. Here, they found that the rear window had been shattered, not by the crash, but by the bullets fired by the law enforcement contingent. Mike reached down on the floor and felt around until he found his bag. They slowly crawled up and over the rear seat back and out through the shattered window opening. As they crawled up and across the trunk, they realized that the car was practically standing on end. It was also shifting and jiggling and swaying on the cables that were suspending it high above the river bank. By using the broken window framing for footing support, they were able to stand up and reach over the back end of the trunk lid and find a hand-hold on the bottom edge of the trunk to pull themselves up and over the back end of their car. Mike went first, sliding down over the bumper and luckily was able to find a foothold on the ground at the edge of the embankment. He carefully helped Audrey down off of the rear end of their car. It was then that they realized that someone was shooting at them from across the highway. They still didn't comprehend what had actually happened with the road-block and everything. The shooters couldn't really see anything in the total darkness and black fog. As some of the bullets began pinging off the metal of the rear underside of their car that was still sticking above the embankment, the two snowbirds quickly got down on their stomachs and began crawling along the narrow shoulder space on the outside of the cable guardrail. After they had crawled about fifty yards along the edge of the embankment, they noticed that the gunfire increased as more people were joining in the foray.

Back across the highway, the two cartel agents who had been sitting in their car up to now; suddenly jumped out to join in the shootout. They at first didn't want to get involved in the capture of the two escapees. They wanted to come in at the end and lay claim to the drugs and money that they were sure were theirs in the back of the Impala. But, now, the lure of the gunfight drew them out to join in. They came around behind the Sheriff and the FBI and DEA officers and joined in firing in the same direction. One could guess with certainty that with all that firepower, eventually one of the bullets would hit the gas tank of the upturned vehicle. Sure enough, very soon one did. There was a huge ball of fire which blew the Impala to smithereens and lit up the entire area in spite of the heavy fog.

In that sudden huge flash of light, the law enforcement contingent suddenly realized that there were people behind them also firing at the car, that were not part of their law group. They turned and began shooting at the two strangers. One of the cartel agents went down, dead immediately. The other one opened fire on the Sheriff and other two law officers, taking all three of them out. The cartel agent also went down with a crippling bullet wound.

As the blazing ball of fire of the Impala fell into the chasm and the gunfire subsided, the area became deathly quiet as total darkness and the fog again enveloped the scene.

After about a minute of the silence, Mike whispered to Audrey, "I think they're all dead. We better get out of here."

With that the both got to their feet and carefully crossed the highway to where the flash of light had exposed the cartel car. This was their lucky night. The two cartel guys who had been sitting in their car waiting until they decided to get into the battle, had left the car running to de-fog the windows. Mike opened the car door and tossed his bag in, and our snowbirds climbed in and took off. They drove carefully through the sleeping town of Longview, Washington and out to the entrance to I-5, North.

They drove along quietly at first, still in shock and puzzlement from their near-death experience. Finally, they realized that they had to talk about it, because now they had an entirely new set of problems.

“What the heck just happened back there?” Mike asked in a rhetorical question.

“I don’t know, but I think we are lucky to be alive.”

“Who the heck were those people? And, how did they know we were coming across that bridge tonight?”

“I think that someone has been following us all along and feeding our information to the FBI and DEA.”

“I agree, I think it was those cartel guys. The same ones who broke into our motel room back in Oregon. Maybe one of them was actually a mole for the FBI, working for the Medellin Drug Cartel.”

“Well, they’re all probably dead now. We can only hope; killed in that crazy shootout back there on that bridge..”

“Yeah, and maybe they’ll think that we also died when our car exploded and crashed into the Columbia River.”

The two snowbirds lapsed into silence again. There wasn't much more they could say about it. They were alive and other people were dead. Not entirely their fault. It would take authorities weeks, if not months to sort through all the carnage and wreckage of that shoot out, both on and off of that bridge. They sped on into the night in silence, stopping for coffee, potty and gas at a truck stop in Chehalis, Washington. At that point, they knew not what lied ahead. They didn't really have any further plans, just to get to Seattle and find a place to sleep. They were both dead tired from their ordeal on the Longview Bridge.

FREEDOM

Carlotta quickly opened the letter and found five passports inside. One for herself and one for each of the children: Juanita, Madeline, Juan and Antonio. Her own two young children, the twins, Jose and Christina would not need passports, only their birth certificates. She looked at the clock; it's still early. She called Angelina as soon as Angelina got home from work. She realizes that she will have to talk in code; the phone was probably bugged.

"I've received the material in the mail that we talked about."

"Oh, that's good, let me make arrangements for our meeting. I'll call you back."

An hour later, Angelina called back. All she said, was, "Three days after Antonio's birthday, at five A.M., my house. Bring only the clothes you wear."

After she hung up from Angelina, Carlotta again got her shopping bags and headed for the market. She can't drop off the twins, Jose and Christina at the sitter's with such short notice, so they come with this time. After she purchased just a few items, she again found the small secret alcove with the pay phone. She ushered the children into a corner and gave them each a carrot to munch on to occupy them. With the correct pesos dropped into the slot the phone rang in Las Vegas. Lucita Adriana answered her phone.

"Two days after Antonio's birthday," Carlotta says, but suddenly realizes she is talking in code and Lucita would have no idea what she was talking about, or who she was.

"I'm sorry Lucita, this is Carlotta. I've made arrangements to get us to El Paso. We should be getting there in about five days."

"Oh, wonderful, Carlotta. I'm so glad you called. Joseppi and I are already packed. We have been in a panic. Joseppi said he saw a black Mercedes drive by our house several times yesterday, and this morning that same black Mercedes followed him to work. He says that is the standard car that the drug cartel drives. Believe me, no one drives a Mercedes in this neighborhood unless they are drug people. We are so scared, Carlotta. We can't wait to get out of here."

"Okay Lucita, tell me where we should meet you and Joseppi in El Paso

"As I understand it, the bus from the DELCO plant in Juarez will cross the border near the town of Socorra, south of El Paso and proceed to the U.S. town of Tornillo to drop off DELCO workers. We will meet you there, at that bus stop in five days. You have my cell phone number if there is a change of plans.. We'll be driving a silver colored SUV called the Suburban."

"We'll see you here in five days Lucita. Thank you so much.. How will we ever repay you and Joseppi for all you've done for us."

"Well, I fear that my sister Maria is dead and I will do whatever I can for those dear children of hers. They are the only family I have left."

They both hung up and Carlotta gathered up her two little twins and headed back home.

* * * * * *

In downtown Las Vegas, ninth floor of the Nevada building, Rickardo Denosa was sitting down with Francesco Ramirez. They have just finished listening to a tap on the phone of Lucita and Joseppi Adriana.

"Good work, Francesco. Now we're getting somewhere. Looks like the whole damn bunch is heading for El Paso. Get your ass down there and meet them when they get off that DELCO bus. Set up an interrogation room in that old motel where you've done the other one's and go to work on them and don't stop until you get some answers. Get that lazy bastard Juan Carlos to join you. He usually has good results. If he hadn't backed off last time, we would have some answers by now. Maybe he can follow them across the border in Juarez and make sure they get to the rendezvous."

* * * * * *

The bus from Chihuahua to Juarez was right on time, at five A.M. The four Mendoza children, their step mom, Carlotta and her own two children Jose and Christina, left their home with only the clothes that they wore that morning. Juanita had, in her purse, the money that their father and mother had left behind. Along with Carlotta's new friend Angelina, they were all on board. It would be about a five hour bus ride. They had packed sandwiches and bottled water. It was still very early, especially for the little ones, the twins. They fall back to sleep after about twenty minutes. The other children, the teens and pre-teens were wide awake and discussing their plight.

"I'm so scared about leaving," Juanita said, "We were just getting settled into our school. We were just starting to make friends. Who knows when we'll even go to school again and make new friends."

"I know," Madeline agrees, "Now we'll never see our friends again. This really sucks. It's all because of that evil cartel with its God-awful drugs. Why are there even drugs in this world?"

"We had to give up everything," Juan says, "All because of that evil cartel. I was just starting to get good at soccer. My coach said I would probably have made the team this year."

"My friends all said we'll be lucky if we live to get across the border to the USA," Juanita adds, "If we don't get shot first and killed by the US border guards and hunted down by the cartel. Some of my friends have been caught and arrested and were forced to return here to Mexico, and they spent time in jail for trying to escape to the USA. It's all very scary. I'll be so terrified until we find some place safe to live in the US."

"I'm so sorry it has to end up this way, children," Carlotta tried to console them, "I do so wish there was another way. But you do realize that if we stay, we will all be killed by that Medellin cartel. We have to get out now. There is no safe place in Mexico anymore from that murdering cartel."

The bus stopped in the town of Estacion Sueco, the half-way point. Everyone got out to stretch their legs and to potty and to eat lunch. The Mendoza group got out for potty, but returned to the bus for their lunch of sandwiches. They arrived at the Delco factory in Juarez at about two P.M. Angelina led them over to the factory bus stop.

While they were waiting for the bus. Juanita suddenly whispers to her step mom, "He's here, Mom! It's him! I'd recognize him anywhere after what he did to me, - - - and to Dad."

"Who's here?" Angelina asks.

"It's that cartel guy that beat me up so badly and raped me and murdered our father," she replied in a whisper with wide-eyed fear.

"I see him too," Carlotta whispered, "what the heck is he doing here. Has he come to kill us all when we get on that bus? We're not getting on that bus with him. Please Angelina, get us all someplace safe, - - - now."

"Okay," Angelina whispers to them, "Follow me."

She led them to the entrance to the factory and shows the security guard her employee pass. They all show their ID's and quickly enter the factory. The man who had, several days ago, come to their house and introduced himself as Juan Carlos, then killed their father and tortured and raped Juanita tried to follow them into the DELCO factory. He was turned away by the security guards because he did not have an employee pass.

Inside the factory Angelina led her group to a visitor's lounge while she went to get her husband Donaldo. She introduced them to Donaldo Hernandez and explained the situation they were in.

"I think I can help you get across to the U.S." he said in a whisper. I have helped many others this way before when they couldn't get on the factory bus for whatever reason. Wait here until we start loading today's run of batteries onto the railroad cars."

The group of refugees waited about two hours. Meanwhile Angelina went to the cafeteria with some money Juanita had given her. She purchased seven large box lunches and fourteen bottles of water. She gave one meal and two waters to each of the children and Carlotta. She said good-bye to them and Carlotta hugged her and thanked her again.

"I will never forget what you have done for us."

Donaldo came back in and told them that it was time. His crew was on their lunch break. They followed him into the factory, all the way to the back, to the loading docks, after stopping at the bathrooms first. There were rows and rows and stacks of large shipping crates ready for loading into the railroad cars. Two of the crates remained empty. He directed the four Mendoza children to get into one of the large crates , and Carlotta and little Jose and Christina Ramirez into the other one...They all took their food and water and climbed into the crates.

Donaldo then gave them instructions. "I must warn you; once we close the crates, no talking, - - absolute silence, especially at the border crossing. There will be border guards inspecting the rail cars. They may or may not inspect yours. They inspect at random. Remember, absolute silence at the border and again when the train gets to the switch yard north of El Paso. If you have to relieve yourselves, you'll have to do so through the slats in the bottom of the pallets. I'm sorry, that's the only way. It may get smelly at times. You'll be in there for two or three days. This is your only ticket to the USA and freedom."

"May I ask," Carlotta asks, "Where are we going to end up?"

"This car load of batteries is headed to San Antonio, Texas. There is a large warehouse there where you will be unloaded. One of the warehouse workers will open your crate and get all of you to a refugee shelter. From there you may be transferred to another city. maybe Dallas, St. Louis, Chicago, or Minnesota."

In a few minutes they heard a loud buzzer sound and Donaldo's crew returned from their break. The crew began loading boxes of the batteries into the Mendoza's and Carlotta's crates.. They stacked the boxes in a wall pattern around the inside edges of their crates completely surrounding them and sealing them in with a crate cover. The batteries had no acid in them, of course. All batteries are shipped dry. The crates were made of heavy wooden slats with four wood blocks attached to the bottom for the forklift bars to slide under when moving and stacking the crates. There were small spaces between the slats and the loaders had left small openings between some of the battery boxes so they could get air in and see out, somewhat. The empty batteries were not very heavy so the crates were fairly large, about four by six feet and four feet high. Soon they were loaded into the box car. Their crates were loaded first, so to be on the bottom row, They were less likely to be inspected there. Another row of battery crates was stacked on top of theirs and the boxcar doors closed and locked. In a short while, the train began to move. It was a fairly long train with five boxcars of the DELCO batteries and twenty or so box cars of auto parts followed by about ten car hauling cars from assembly plants near Mexico City. The train moved slowly up to the border crossing, then stopped on the U.S. side as cargo and manifests were checked for accuracy. Some of the cars were inspected at random, but not the DELCO car with the refugees inside.

The train moved rapidly from the border crossing to a large switchyard northeast of El Paso. Here the cars were separated from the engine and turned over to the Union Pacific Railroad and the engine returned to Mexico. The cars of the train were also then split up. The car hauler cars and the cars of automotive parts were split up. Some were going west to assembly plants in California and some to Midwest and East Coast assembly plants. The battery hauling cars were switched to a train bound for San Antonio, Texas. That train, however had to wait there a whole day. It waited for cars coming in from California, from the Los Angeles port, container cars of merchandise of all sorts bound for the Midwest, South and East Coast. The refugees grew tired and bored and soon fell asleep, exhausted from the stressful day of being uprooted from their home and driven out of their homeland by the devil cartel.

* * * * * *

That devil with the name Juan Carlos, after being refused entry into the DECO factory, boarded the factory bus and was transported across the border to El Paso. It was no big deal for him, crossing the border. He was back and forth countless times doing work for the Mendellin drug cartel; disguised as a U.S. Customs Agent. Juan got off the bus in downtown El Paso and gave his friend Vasquez a call. They met at the El Paso's cartel office.

"I've got some work for you," He told Vasquez, "Maybe some wet work,"

"Oh, I love the wet work you bring me. Just tell me where and when."

"Come with me right now. You can start today. It's right here in town."

Juan checked out a company van; thinking that the Mendoza's will also be at the bus stop. The two cartel hit men drove to the suburb of Tornillo, to the bus stop where he thought the two friends of Carlotta would be waiting. He knew this from a call he received from the cartel office in Las Vegas, after the phone tap on Joseppi and Lucita's phone.

The DELCO bus dropped off workers at the bus stop in Tornillo. Joseppi and Lucita watched all the workers get off the bus. Joseppi held up a picture they brought of Carlotta, but they didn't see anyone resembling her picture, nor did they see any young children get off the bus.

"Oh dear, it looks like they didn't make it on this bus," Lucita comments to Joseppi.

"Well maybe we'll just have to wait around for the next bus. Meantime, maybe she'll call."

Juan Carlos saw the man holding up a picture of Carlotta and approached Joseppi and Lucita.

"I see you have been waiting for Carlotta and the kids."

"Yes we have, but it looks like she missed the bus."

"Well I just came across the border on that bus. I saw them get off at the Fabens stop. We told Carlotta we would run down here and pick you up and bring you back to Fabens where they are waiting," he lied, "Come get in the van and we'll take you over to Fabens."

Joseppi and Lucita got into the back of the van. After Juan drove a short ways, he pulled over and stoped the van. He turned around in his seat and showed them his false Customs Agent badge.

"I'm going to have to take you in for questioning. I believe you are involved in bringing illegal Mexicans into the U.S."

He handcuffed them both and drove them to a very old secluded abandoned motel a ways off of I Ten on the outskirts of El Paso. The room still had a bed, but no bedding on it. The entire building had a certain smell about it. One would call it the stench of death. The motel had not been used for over fifty years. The city had condemned it back when the freeway was built, but could not sell the property because of zoning laws that had to be changed. No one realized that half the rooms had dead bodies in them, the work of Juan and Vazquez. Mostly a result of their. 'training and indoctrination of drug mules'. to bring the cartel's drugs across the border into the U.S. It didn't take long for Joseppi and Lucita to realize what's going to happen to them and that they probably won't be leaving there alive.

Juan Carlos unlocked and opened the motel room door and the two cartel thugs shoved Joseppi and Lucita in and threw them down on the bed.

"Now, we will talk," Juan yelled at them.

"Who the hell are you, and what do you want with us?" Joseppi yelled back at him.

Juan took his gun and smacked him across the face, breaking several teeth and bloodying his lip and nose.

"Shut the hell up. I'll be the one doing the talking and asking the questions here. I want information on your friend Carlotta and her kids. We think those Mendoza kids have information about a shipment of cartel drugs and the cartel wants to know what happened to their drugs."

"We don't know anything about your drug shipment," Lucita says.

Juan took his gun and whipped it across Lucita's face, breaking her nose and gashing her upper cheek open as she fell back onto the bed bleeding.

"No, no, stupid bitch, I didn't ask you about the drug shipment. I want to know about those damn kids. I think they know something about the shipment. Now, I know they were just about to board the bus, but they spotted me and ran into the DELCO factory. I need to know how they are going to get across the border and where they were going to meet up with you. Are they going to meet up with you back at your place in Vegas?"

"No," Joseppi replies, "We sold our house in Vegas before we came here to El Paso."

"Well, you must have a plan as to where you all were going after they net up with you at the bus stop."

Joseppi and Lucita won't say another word, even after another hour of beatings. Finally Juan and Vacquez leave, saying they are going out to dinner. They leave them bloody, beaten and unconscious, tied up and gagged. Joseppi and Lucita come to sometime in the morning and realize their tormentors have not returned. Through broken teeth and swollen lips they try to talk through their gags.

"They'll probably go to the bus stop again to see if Carlotta and the children have gotten on the next day's bus," Joseppt says.

"I really hope they don't get on any of those busses," Lucita says, "They'll surely be dead if they do."

"How much longer do you think we can hold out?"

"I don't know, let's see if they come back with Carlotta and the kids."

The two tortured prisoners fall silent again, either asleep or back into unconsciousness. Later that afternoon, Juan and Vasquez wait for the DELCO bus.

"If the kids are on this bus, do I get to go back and kill those other two?"

"Yeah, probably, they'll be of no use to us if we get the kids."

"Yeah, I'll like that. How about after the kids talk? I've never killed kids before. It'll be fun," Vasquez says as he grins through several broken front teeth.

Joseppi and Lucita are awakened by the door being opened. Their gags are removed and hands and feet untied. They are allowed to go to the bathroom and are each given a bottle of water and they down it.

"We've got to keep you alive until you talk or we get the kids," Juan informs them.

They again refuse to talk and are again are used as punching bags.

"You have one more day. If we don't get the kids, then you talk or you die," Juan says as they tie their prisoners up again and leave.

"I don't think I can take much more of this," Lucita says.

"Well, if you can hang on just a little longer, I have a plan," Joseppi says.

Again, before they pass out; through their broken jaws and swollen lips they do their best to discuss their plan.

The third day, the same results; no kids on the bus. The tortured prisoners are again awakened by the door being unlocked. But they are relieved when there's no kids. The two captors each put a gun to the prisoners heads.

"Okay," Juan says as they undo the gags, "It's time to talk or die."

"Alright, alright," Lucita says, "We were all going to Denver. Maybe that's where they headed."

"So, where in Denver," Juan asks.

"At my sister's place," Joseppi answers.

"So, give me the damn address."

"It's 8801 York Street North."

"It's about damn time we get some results. Vasquez, you can finish up here. I'll meet you in the car. Lock up when you finish.

Juan leaves and closes the motel room door. The two prisoners began saying their last prayers as they prepare to meet their God. Vasquez raises his gun and silently thinks, "Finally, after three days, I get to kill someone."

He looks at Joseppi and Lucita and as he pulls the trigger on Joseppi, he notices that Joseppi has turned his head and is smiling at Lucita and Lucita is smiling back at Joseppi; painfully, through swollen, battered lips. These smiles they will carry with them into the hereafter and will share it for all eternity.

As Vasquez pulls the trigger on Lucita, he was deeply troubled by the smiles. Never before had anyone he was murdering, been smiling. He closed and locked the door and as he walked to the car, he was still puzzling over the smiles. He got in the car and Juan told him he would drop him off at the office and he would head to Denver.

Meanwhile, back inside the old abandoned motel room; as the last few seconds of life slipped away, there is a peace unlike any other. The reason Joseppi and Lucita were smiling at each other was that they had; even in death, outsmarted the Medellin Drug Cartel. The address they gave Juan Carlos was an old abandoned warehouse on Denver's North Side. Joseppi has no sister in Denver; and at this very moment five hundred and fifty four miles east, in San Antonio, Carlotta and the children were being released from their crates.

* * * * * *

The train moves east, ever east through the night, across Texas. In it's bowels it carries a cargo of precious humanity. Like two tiny seed pods blowing on the wind. Each seed waiting to find fertile soil in this rich land; to take root and grow into a beautiful tree, becoming productive and producing nutritious fruit. Like the countless millions before them, they are cast upon our shores, escaping the tyranny and persecution in their homeland. Filled with hope for a better life in a country who's government offers its citizens at least a glimmer of hope of controlling their own destiny and improving the life of all of its citizens.

HOMELESS AND HOMESICK IN SEATTLE

Awakened at six A.M. by the loud, shrill, screeching roar of jet engines, Mike leaps out of bed.

"What the heck is that?" he questions no one, because Audrey is still sleeping through the roar, "It sounds like we were asleep on an airport runway."

He's pretty close to right. The motel they had chosen is right next door to the Sea Tac Airport. While he is showering, he has this idea. He gets dressed and heads downstairs to the breakfast buffet. As he is eating his breakfast, he watches the morning news on the dining room TV. They are talking about the shootout on the Longview Bridge. The reporter is saying that there was one survivor from all the carnage.

"This person, who's identity is still unknown was in critical condition after being air-lifted to a Portland hospital."

"Oh no!" Mike thinks, almost out loud, "That means that it won't take the authorities long at all to realize he and Audrey didn't die in the shootout."

He hurriedly finishes his breakfast and gets back to the room and wakes up Audrey. After she is fully awake and showered and dressed, he explains to her what he saw on the morning news in the breakfast room.

"We've got to get out of here, now," was her initial reaction, "But where do we go."

"First we need to get rid of that car that we borrowed from whomever at the shootout on the Longview Bridge. We don't even know who it belongs to. It won't take the police long to issue an APB on it, if they already haven't. I was thinking that as long as we are this close to the airport, we could just drive it into an airport parking ramp and after wiping it clean of our finger prints and DNA, we can just leave it there.

"Okay, good plan, Mike. Let's get going. We don't have a minute to spare," Audrey says now in a full panic mode, "For once I'm actually glad we don't have any clothes, or anything to pack. All our stuff got blown up in that big ball of fire at the bridge."

Mike grabs his shoulder bag and they quickly check out and drive the car over to one of the long-term parking ramps. After wiping it down, they leave it and enter the terminal. Here they immediately realize that there are cameras everywhere. They will need some kind of disguises. They find a gift shop and discreetly purchase hooded sweat shirts. After finding bathrooms, they slip into the hoodies. Lucky for them the airport is really crowded at this time of the morning. They re-enter the crowded flow of passengers with their hoods up. As they move through the main terminal, Audrey spots a wig salon. The fugitives duck into the salon and very discretely purchase ready-made wigs and makeup to wear. Back into another bathroom and out again as two different people, thankful for the throngs of people. They find a sit-down Starbucks and take a break with spendy beverages.

"Now what?" Audrey asks, "Seeing how we are now living in George Orwell's 1949 dystopian novel, 1984, where cameras are watching you everywhere you go and everybody knows everything about everybody."

"Yes, it's a sad end this world is coming to. The word 'privacy' is fast becoming an obsolete concept."

"We need to escape this nightmare, once and for all. Here's an idea; how about we purchase tickets to someplace far away, outside the U.S. But then we don't actually get on the plane. Wouldn't that throw them off our trail?"

"That sounds like a plan that might really work. We could use our old ID's to get the tickets, then find someone to give the tickets and ID's to. That way there would be someone actually getting on a plane with those tickets."

"Okay, let's do it. How about tickets to Seoul, Korea? We'll first have to un-disguise ourselves, then get the tickets, then put the disguises back on while we find someone who wants to go to Seoul, Korea."

So, back into the bathrooms to get 'un-disguised'. At the ticket machines, they used their old California drivers licenses and made sure they were spotted by the surveillance cameras. Back into the bathrooms they went, to don the disguises again.

"With all the costume changing," Audrey comments, "I'm beginning to think we are in show business."

"Yeah, me too. Oh look, Honey, there's a soldier and his wife or girlfriend, probably bound for South Korea. The U.S. still has a large contingent of troops stationed in South Korea, and, as I recall, SeaTac is the departure point for G.I's going over there."

They approached the soldier and his wife.

“Excuse me, Sergeant,” Mike said, “Are you by chance headed for South Korea?”

“Yes sir, we are. Are you selling something? We are in a big hurry here. We’re late for our flight.”

“Do you have your tickets yet?”

“No, sir we don’t. We’ve been home on emergency leave and haven’t had time to get them yet.”

“And now we’re running out of time,” His wife says, “And money,” she adds.

“Well, here’s the thing,” Mike says, “We have two tickets to Seoul which we can’t use. We were scheduled for a business meeting there tomorrow. Only our company called just now and cancelled the meeting. Here, why don’t you take these,” He says as he hands them the pair of tickets, “The only caveat is you’ll also need these ID’s.”

Audrey hands them the fake ID’s, “Just mail these back to us at this address,” She also hands them a slip of paper with their Minnesota address on it.

“Oh, my God, Honey,” the wife said to the soldier, “This is truly a miracle, To Mike and Audrey, she says; “How can we ever thank you?”

“It’s okay, I was a soldier once upon a time too. Now, go, go, get on that flight.”

As the soldier couple runs off, Mike walked over to the ticket counter and asked the ticket agent to hold up the flight to Seoul. "There's a soldier and his wife with an emergency trying to get to the gate for that flight."

The ticket agent picked up his phone and called the gate with the departure for Seoul and told them to hold the flight for a few minutes, for a soldier and his wife running to make the flight.

"Now that's what I call a win, win, Mike says. "They needed a ticket real fast and we needed to be on that flight."

"Good job, Honey, now let's get out of here while our disguises still work. But where to now?"

* * * * * *

267 Washington Avenue, Federal Building, Las Vegas. FBI District Director Rick Nelson is speaking to a meeting of special agents. Among them is DEA Special Agent Roger Morgan.

"Ladies and gentlemen, I am sorry to report to you that we have lost two of our finest field agents last night, one FBI and one DEA. They were killed in a sting operation near the town of Longview, Washington. They had set up a road block on the Columbia River Bridge to stop drug running suspects from passing from Oregon into Washington. Four local Law Enforcement personnel also lost their lives, including the local Sheriff."

"What happened?" Asks one of the special agents.

"Well, we don't have all of the facts yet, obviously. But it appears that a heavy fog coming up the Columbia River Gorge enveloped the road block. The two suspects, not seeing the road block, crashed into one of the local patrol cars, carrying it through the cables of the guard rail and over the fifty foot embankment to the river bank below. The crash took three members of the SWAT team down with it. The suspect's car also went into the guard rail cables. A gun fight ensued, resulting in the suspects' car exploding and plunging through the cables to the river shore below."

"So, how did our agents die?" Askes another agent.

"After the suspect's car exploded, the gun fight continued as several drug cartel members arrived on the scene and engaged our agents. They probably were also after the drugs in the suspect's car. The result of the gunfight with the cartel was the death of our two agents, and of the local Sheriff."

"What happened to the cartel?"

"One of the cartel agents was killed in the gunfight. Another is in critical condition at a Portland hospital. We believe that a third cartel agent fled the scene in their vehicle. We are currently tracking down that vehicle."

"So, the drug running suspects are also dead?"

"Yes, killed in their car as it exploded and plunged into the river gorge. There was nothing but charred metal at the rivers edge down below. So we are closing the file on them. Operation 'Snowbirds" is officially over."

"What about those cartel agents that showed up and killed our two agents?"

"Oh, it is not over for them. We will be pursuing that third cartel person that fled the scene."

"How did they find out about our sting operation and that roadblock?"

"Gentlemen, all I can say right now is; I believe we have a mole."

* * * * * *

The Uber pulled out of the Sea Tac airport and got on the 405 freeway and headed north along the shores of Lake Washington to the suburb of Bellevue. The snowbirds had asked the driver to take them to a shopping mall. He chose the Factoria Mall., just off the 405 and I 90 in Bellevue. The two snowbirds stepped out of the Uber into a beautiful sunny summer day in Seattle. It is mid-June, the rainy season is over and the sun is shining.

"Boy, oh boy," Audrey says, "I can't wait to finally get some new clothes. Seems like I've been in these same clothes for months. We lost everything in that fiery explosion on that bridge."

"I totally agree, Honey, maybe we can even get out of these ridiculous disguises. But first things first. We need to get some new electronics so we can find out what's going on back home, and if and when it's safe for us to return."

The Best Buy Store offered just what they needed. First they purchased two I-Pad lap tops.

While they had the Geek Squad initialize them and charge the batteries, they headed for the cell phone section. They each got a new I-Phone and had them initialized and charged. When everything was set up and charged they headed for the Food Court. After they wolfed down huge platters of Chipotles, they made calls back home to Minnesota.

"What the heck is going on, Dad," son Chris asked, "There was an FBI agent here recently, wanting to know if we had seen or heard from you. What should I tell him if he comes back?"

"Oh, I don't think they'll be back. We were involved in a very bad accident and one of the cars had a lot of drugs in it. But they probably think we're dead now. We're not, of course, but, if they do come back, you haven't heard from us and this conversation never happened."

He gave Chris their new phone number and told him to call right away if the FBI returns. Next he called daughter Heidi and gets the same story. He told her also, about the accident and the FBI thinking they are dead. He told her to not tell anyone they are still alive.

"Are you guys okay? I mean after the car accident and everything? When are you coming home?"

"I don't know for sure yet. We've got to wait for our insurance claim to go through. We'll be in touch when we head home."

Meanwhile, Audrey called daughter Linda,

"Oh Mom, I've been so worried about you and Dad. What's going on? Are you guys alright?"

"Yes, Honey, we're fine now. But we were involved in a car accident and our car was totaled. We have to wait now for an insurance settlement before we can get a new car and head home."

"But why is the FBI involved? They were here just yesterday and asked a lot of questions about you guys. Such as, why is your car parked in our driveway? I tried to explain about me not wanting to fly back from Lake Havasu. I don't know if they believed me because they wanted to search the house for you. But they didn't have a warrant to search so they finally left. Did you guys do something illegal?"

"No, but I guess there may have been a question of some drugs in one of the cars involved in the crash. Our car was badly damaged and burned after the crash so they probably now think we were killed and burned. Just let them think that, maybe they'll leave us alone. Don't tell anyone about this call."

Mike called Rachel and relayed the same message and gave her his new phone number and told her to call if anyone asks about them.

Next Audrey called sons Richard and Jeff and explains the same thing to them. She told them also not to tell anyone about hearing from them, especially the FBI. She says they will be home after they get their insurance settlement. Meanwhile, Mike called son Roger and asked if he had heard from the FBI. He told him about the exploding car accident and that the FBI may believe that they were killed.

"Well," Roger begins, "Someone was here asking about you and Audrey, but I don't think it was the FBI. He showed me a badge, but I'm pretty sure it was phony. He asked some questions, but I didn't tell him much of anything."

"Well, if he comes back, call the local FBI, then call me. We'll be home as soon as we get the insurance settlement from our accident."

When they were both finished calling all their children, Mike told Audrey what Roger had told him about the phony FBI agent.

"I'll bet," she said, "That's one of those cartel creeps. I'll bet they were sure that we had some of their drugs from that plane crash. It probably was someone other than the two who were killed in that bridge shootout."

"Yeah, it looks like we can't go home yet; not for a while. The problem is that we don't know for sure that the FBI thinks we are dead. We don't know what they know. If they find that cartel car that we took and left in the airport ramp, they could believe we booked a flight to Korea. But we don't know that for sure.

"Okay then," Audrey said, "Let's go shopping. Right now we have no clean clothes and we don't have a place to live. I saw a Kohls store when we came into this mall. Let's start there."

The two snowbirds headed for the Kohls store. After several hours of shopping, they each had a half dozen new outfits, including socks and underwear. They also purchased some luggage to transport their new clothes in. After their shopping spree they found a fast food restaurant and grabbed some lunch. while they each get out their I Pads and work on finding a place to live.

"Look, there are some cute apartments right here in Bellevue," Audrey says.

"No, I'm sorry Honey, but I don't think we should commit to a long term lease. Hopefully we won't be here very long. I've found several of these residence inns right nearby, right on I 90. We can stay there short term, and they are furnished so we won't need to buy furniture."

They called a Sheraton Inn Suites, then called Uber.

* * * * * *

267 Washington Avenue, Federal Bldg, Las Vegas. FBI district Director Rick Nelson was holding his weekly status meeting. Present were; special agents from the southwest district. Also present is Special Agent Joseph Roncowski from the Seattle area and Special Agent Donald Johnson from Portland.

"Here is an update on that incident on the Longview Washington bridge," Special agent Joseph Roncowski begins, "Our CSI team has gone over the scene on the bridge and down below. Our previous initial findings proved to be mostly true. However after a thorough examination of the suspect's car that exploded, they have found no trace of any drugs in the remains of the car. Further, they did not find any trace of the remains of the two suspects that we were in pursuit of. The conclusions of the CSI team are: one, there were never any drugs in the suspect's car, and two, the two suspects may well have escaped before the car exploded."

Agent Donald Johnson got up next and gave his report on the case.

"I have been following up on the drug cartel person that survived the shootout on the bridge. After almost a month in a coma, he was finally able to talk. He claims that just before he passed out from his gunshot, he saw two people run across the road, away from the exploded car and get into his car and drive off. He said that he had left his car running because of the fog. He gave me a description of his car."

Special Agent Joseph Roncowski of Seattle got up and gave his additional report.

"We followed up on Agent Johnson's story and issued an APB on the car in question. Our computers cross referenced the car with a report of abandoned cars left at the SeaTac airport. We found the car in the ramp, however, it had been wiped clean of any prints or DNA. But we went over footage from cameras inside the airport the day the car was checked into the ramp and found our two suspects buying tickets to Seoul, Korea. The airline's computer showed those tickets were checked on board on the flight to Seoul."

Director Rick Nelson gave his concluding remarks next.

"I have asked INTERPOL to follow up on the suspects in Korea, however they will not put resources on the case without proof that there was an international crime being committed.

Gentlemen, once again, we have no case against these two. We're done spinning our wheels and losing lives over nothing. Let the

Medellin cartel spin their wheels if they want. Our case of the 'Snowbirds' has melted away; pardon the pun. The case of the Snowbirds is once again closed."

* * * * * *

Across town in downtown Las Vegas, in another office high-rise, ninth floor, another status meeting is under way. Rickardo Denosa, Southwest District Director for the Medellin Drug Cartel again slams his hand down on the table to start the meeting. Present were the directors from the six major drug market cities of the west coast, along with cartel Agent Jose Mendosa, the survivor of that infamous bridge shootout. Also present was Special Agent Juan Carlos.

"First let me congratulate you Jose for surviving that gun battle on the Longview bridge. You done good for that, and for remembering seeing those two thieves making a run for it in your car. Here's what I want you to do: head back up there to Seattle; get your car back and check around at the airport. Make sure what the FBI has said is true, that those two have really fled to Seoul, Korea. You're in charge now, of Seattle, after your partner was killed at that bridge. If it looks like they actually left for Korea, get on a plane and follow them. See if they are just on vacation, or are intending to stay there. When you find them, question them, find out what they did with our drugs. You see, gentlemen, I don't believe the FBI when they said there were never any drugs in that car. Maybe true, there weren't drugs in the car when it exploded. I believe that they had stashed our drugs somewhere before they drove across that bridge. We need to find out where. I want you city area directors all the way from L.A. to Seattle checking for the cache that they stashed somewhere, or possibly sold the whole batch in bulk to some broker."

Juan, you're our agent at large. I'm really pissed off at you for what happened in Juarez.. I should just have you eliminated which is what we would normally do to someone who has failed in their assignment. You lost track of the Mendoza kids at that DELCO factory. They would have been key to finding where our drug shipment went. And then you got suckered into going to Denver looking for them after that couple set you up on a wild goose chase. Here's the deal. I'm offering you a chance to redeem yourself. Mostly because we're short on agents right now. I want you to get up to Minnesota and keep your eye on the home of those two snowbirds that stole our drugs, in case they return to their home after their little vacation in Korea. Don't fail me on this assignment or you're a dead man, got it?'

"Yes sir, and thank you for another chance. I won't fail you on this, or I'll die trying."

"You damn right you won't. Now, get your butt out of here and report back to me weekly."

Rickardo slams his hand down again and yells at the staff of cartel agents;

"That's all, so get the hell out there and find our drug shipment. Bogota is waiting, they're getting impatient."

* * * * * *

The Union Pacific switch engine pushes the four cars of batteries into the huge DELCO warehouse in the outskirts of San Antonio, Texas. The brakes are locked, the engine backs out and the doors are closed. The railroad car doors are unlocked and an army of forklift drivers go to work. The batteries were packed by size and category. There are very huge batteries that go into forklifts and other heavy lifting machines. There are medium batteries for medium vehicles such as golf carts and scooters. Then there are the regular sized automotive sized batteries for cars and trucks. The batteries are stored also by category and size. At the front of the warehouse battery orders are fulfilled. Most of the batteries are ordered by the manufacturers of the above mentioned equipment. The largest volume of orders go to the automotive industry, to their plants in the Detroit area, of course, but also Ohio, New Jersey, St Louis, Wisconsin and west coast assembly plants. The acid for all of the batteries is also manufactured in Mexico, but shipped separately and stored in a separate section of the warehouse.

Around the clock, batteries come in and orders are shipped out. The batteries flow through this huge warehouse like a river, non-stop, twenty-four-seven.

After about an hour, the four train cars are unloaded and the last car hosed down. The warehouse doors are opened. The switch engine pulls out the four empty cars and replaces them with several full ones. The pallets that contain our refugees are taken to a special secluded section of the dock. These will be hand unpacked by juniors, of beginning dock workers just learning the system. Most of this crew knows what to expect when they open the crates. The stench is almost overwhelming. These poor refugees have been sealed in the crates for over three days without any bathroom facilities but to relieve themselves through the slats in the bottom of their crates. They had been given but one full meal to last the three days and two of the sixteen ounce bottles of water each. The refugees need to be helped to climb out of their crates, they are so cramped and stiff from sitting with their knees up under their chins, day and night for three days, but they consider this a small price to pay for freedom.

* * * * * *

These refugees are the lucky ones. By far, the vast majority of refugees will attempt to escape the tyranny of Mexico on their own. They will attempt to cross the border at night, crawling through the barbed wire and brush and prickly cactus on their bellies to avoid the search lights of the U.S. Border patrol. They are hunted down by dogs. Some are beaten and raped and shot. Some will die in the hot desert sun. Some will die from dehydration and malnutrition. Some are captured and imprisoned and then sent back to the tyranny of Mexico. The ones who make it through may end up in a refugee center and even find a job and try to make a living only to find years later that because they are considered 'illegal', they are arrested and sent back. Many families are split up and parents are unable to find their children because of the language barrier between English and Spanish.

You may ask yourself, how can this happen; in a country that was founded and built by refugees. How can we not find a better way of helping these refugees. We pay our politicians exorbitant amounts of money to solve these political and social problems. How can they not find solutions?

President Trump thinks he has the solution; build a wall. That didn't work too well for Berlin, did it? Maybe it's the U.S. that's headed for collapse, as was the USSR in the nineteen seventies.

* * * * * *

The crates are then hosed down and reloaded onto the boxcars and returned to the factory.

A social worker from the refugee center mission greets them.

"Welcome to the USA and to San Antonio. My name is Delores," she says in Spanish.

Carlotta corrects her and informs her that she and the children all speak English. They are first escorted to the employee locker rooms. Here they shower and are given clean clothes from the mission. Next, they are led to the cafeteria for their first hot meal in almost a week, complements of the DELCO Battery Company. The company supports the program of rescuing refugees from Mexico. Many of the thousand or so employees of the warehouse were refugees themselves and are now Green Card holders. Many other companies that have moved a lot of their manufacturing functions to Mexico are realizing that they must work at improving the economic condition of the country that provides them the manpower to run their factories. This means helping the people who need to leave the country due to the over-crowding and impoverishment of the ones who cannot be employed by these manufacturing facilities, And also those who are being persecuted and driven out by the ruthless and savage drug cartels.

After Carlotta and the Mendoza and Ramirez children were finished eating, they were escorted to the employee lounge, they waited until the end of the day shift when buses would take many of the employees and new refugees downtown to the shelter. Here they were given beds, clothing and food while they waited to be transported to one of the Midwestern cities.

THE RETURN OF THE SNOWBIRDS

Days turn into weeks and weeks into months as summer soon fades away into autumn. The snow caps on Washington's peaks become brighter and larger with new snow and the forested valleys are once again painted with the brilliant and varied colors of a new autumn season. As the days grow shorter and shorter and in 'The City of The King', the beautiful harbor city on the Sound, the sunny days become fewer and fewer as the fog once again rolls in down the Puget Sound from the chilling Pacific Ocean. This river of fog flows in without even a whisper and rapidly fills the famous sound with a soft blanket that silences the great city. This river of fog flows in, past the towns of Port Townsend and Oak Harbor, guarding the sound on the north. It flows past the long and beautiful island of Whidby, down to the ferry boat harbor of Mukiteo. It flows on past the famous landmark; the Space Needle, standing there like the king's scepter, guarding the realm on the north. The fog blanket buries the cities of Seattle, Bremerton and Tacoma and all the way down to Olympia.

Audrey and Mike, our two snowbirds grow increasingly antsy and begin discussing the possibility of going home to Minnesota. They haven't heard anything more about the Longview Bridge incident, and began to assume that everyone was dead except them. They hadn't heard anything back from their children; so they assumed that the FBI had written them off as killed on the bridge.

The AMTRAK was their transport of choice; there being still a fair amount of caution, albeit paranoia about the more popular means, namely flying. Audrey called daughter Linda and gave her a heads-up that they were coming home to Minnesota. Early one late October morning, under a thick blanket of fog, the displaced couple made their way into downtown Seattle. They boarded the train at the Kings Street Station. A very comfortable Pullman coach carried them halfway across the American continent. In three days they arrived in Saint Paul, Minnesota. Linda picked them up in their own Honda SUV.

"I can't began to tell you how glad I am to see you," she says, "I have been worried sick about you guys since that FBI guy was here and you called about your accident on that bridge. Did you get your insurance claim settled?"

"Oh, yes," Mike had to lie because they didn't dare even file a claim for fear the FBI would trace it.

They stayed at Linda's house for several days, just so they could see their great granddaughters; Kira and McKenna. The girls were absolutely adorable in their Halloween costumes. They leave after making plans with all their children to get together for Thanksgiving and Christmas. Under heavy grey and threatening November skies, the two snowbirds head for their lake home.. They head north through St. Cloud and Brainerd to their home on Thunder Lake. As they get north of St. Cloud, a light snow begins to fall. By the time they get north of Brainerd, it is snowing heavily and there is almost a foot of snow by the time they pull into their driveway and nearly get stuck.

"Well, it looks like we've come full circle, Honey. We left in a snowstorm and a year later we come home to one."

"I know, it's going to feel so good to be home again, to sleep in our own bed."

As they pulled into their garage, Mike says, "Boy, Honey, I don't remember leaving the garage this messy. I'll have to get out here first thing and get this mess cleaned up."

As they enter their house, they are thrown into complete shock.

"What the heck has happened here? Have we been burglarized?" Audrey gasps.

"It kinda looks like someone has gone through here looking for something."

"But what, and who would have destroyed everything like this?"

"I'll bet it was that FBI, looking for the drugs or the money."

"I don't know, Honey. Would they have left such a mess and wrecked the place? We can't even stay here tonight. I'm going to call the county Sheriff and the FBI and find out who would have made such a mess of our house."

"And the Insurance Company. We're going to have to replace everything."

The weary snowbirds get back in their SUV and backtrack to the town of Brainerd and find a motel room for the night. The next morning the snowstorm abates and the plows are out clearing the roads. Mike calls the county Sheriff and the Insurance Company and they all meet at the lake house. The sheriff was the first one there and dusted for finger prints.

"I'll process these prints when I get back to my office. That'll tell us if this was done by anyone with a prior record. These break-ins are becoming more and more common with more snowbirds going away for the winter. My advice; get yourself a security system with a monitoring system. It'll monitor your inside temperature and record anyone breaking in. Put up a lot of signs around the place, warning anyone that they are being photographed. That usually will deter would-be vandals."

The insurance agent went through the house and took pictures of the damage.

"I'll process these pictures and compile a list of your destroyed items and what their replacement values will be. The company will send a check for that amount so you can start shopping for the items to be replaced. Send me a copy of your motel bill for reimbursement. Also, my company will give you a discount for a security system and pay for a clean-up service."

With that, the Insurance Agent left.

"I'll have one of my deputies drive by the house frequently," The Sheriff says, "To deter any further vandalism until you can get your security system installed."

They return to their motel and hire a cleaning crew to come in and clean out all the damaged items from their lake house. In a few weeks they get a check from the insurance company. They spend the next couple days shopping to replace the damaged items and furniture. Mike hires a snowplow contractor to plow out their driveway so the new furniture items can be delivered.

NO HOME FOR OLD PEOPLE

However, when they arrive to meet the delivery truck, they come home to find that the place has been completely destroyed by fire. He calls the local Fire Chief to see if they responded to the fire. The Fire Chief says that they did, but it was middle of the night and the fire had consumed the entire house.

"It looks to me like the fire was an arson I'm afraid. We've found evidence of a gasoline accelerant. Honestly, I've got to ask you at this time, do you have enemies?"

"No, not that I'm aware of," Mike lies, because he is beginning to piece together a picture of who is out to get them.

* * * * * *

Meanwhile in Las Vegas, Rickardo Denosa is on the phone with his special agent Juan Carlos in Minneapolis.

"I have found that couple what stole our drug shipment, Boss. They have returned from Seoul, Korea to their home in the north of Minnesota. I searched their house thoroughly but didn't find the drugs or money, so I torched the place at night hoping to smoke them out so I could question them. But they weren't at home. They come and go so often, it's hard to pin them down. Also it's so damn cold up there in the north. The snow is everywhere. It just keeps coming down every day or so. You can't drive on it, it makes the road so slippery and I get stuck until they plow it off of the roads with these big plows."

"Well, of course it's cold and snowy up there in the north of Minnesota. It's their winter, you idiot. Get used to it. Get yourself some warmer clothes, you know a heavy coat like you see everyone else wearing, and those things they wear on their hands, you know, gloves, and a warm hat, and some boots for walking in the snow."

"Okay boss. I'm hoping that now that I've smoked them out of their house, they don't have a house up in the north anymore. They'll have to live here in Minneapolis. It's a little warmer here in the city."

"You keep after them. When they move into the city, capture them and find out where they've got the drugs and money, then kill them. Keep me posted. Bogota loves updates. Don't freeze to death up there in the north."

* * * * * *

In Minnesota, mid November is sunny and about twenty degrees. In San Antonio, it is sunny and eighty degrees. At the refugee shelter, children were out in the back lot playing a soccer game. As her children were at play, Carlotta was talking with several other parents.

"I heard that very soon we will be transferred out of here," Maria, the mother of two of the young boys playing soccer was saying., "I received a notice this morning from our social worker, Delores. She said to be packed and ready to go in the morning."

"Where are you going?" Carlotta asks.

"I think she said we will be going to Saint Louis, along with eight other refugees."

"I was given notice also," Juanita, mother of two of the older children playing soccer announced, Delores said we would be going to Chicago, along with about ten others. We, too, will be leaving in the morning. How about you Carlotta, what have you heard?"

"Well, I haven't gotten my notice yet," Carlotta replies, "I'm supposed to see Delores right after lunch."

"Do you know what I heard?" Ramone, one of the group going to Denver said, "I heard that after we all leave, they're going to close this center. I heard the Federales are ordering this place closed."

After lunch, Carlotta met with Delores.

"You and your children will be going to Saint Paul, Minnesota," she says, "There will be four other families also going there. We have been trying to get warm clothing for all of you. It's very cold in Minnesota this time of year. Your bus will pick you up early in the morning. Please have all of your children packed up and ready to go."

Duffle bags were handed out to everyone to pack up what little possessions they had. The small bags were purchased from an Army surplus store with funds donated to the shelter. Everyone packed up their things into the duffle bags.

"Mama, does this mean we will be going to our new home now, here in the US," little Antonio asks?

"Well maybe not right away, but soon, maybe we will have a house of our again.

Moments later, one of the shelter staff came in carrying a large duffle bag filled with winter clothes. The winter clothes had been donated and shipped from the St. Paul Salvation Army. Juanita helped her younger siblings try on the donated items. When all of the Mendoza and Ramirez children and also Juanita and Carlotta found coats, hats and mittens that fit them; they all began to laugh at each other.

"We look like Eskimos," Little Antonio said.

""Look at these funny things on our hands," twelve year old Juan remarked, "I've never ever had these kind of things on my hands before. We all look like monsters with huge hands."

"Mama," little Jose and Christina, the twins, age five ask, "Will we have to wear these things all the time in cold Minnesota? What are these things called anyway?"

"Those are called mittens, children, and no, you will only have to wear those when you go outside to play," Carlotta replies.

"I thought you said it was cold everywhere in Minnesota," eight year old Madeline says.

"No, she meant everywhere outside," Juanita corrected her, "It is warm inside. They have artificial heat indoors, like we had at our little mountain home in La Junta."

They all pack the winter clothes into their duffle bags. All of the children in the shelter went to bed with their clothes on. They all went to bed early, knowing they would have to get up very early to get on the busses.

At about three A.M. four school buses pulled up in front of the refugee shelter. Delores, the Social Worker in charge of the shelter came out to greet the bus drivers. She and her staff checked the drivers papers, their drivers licenses and insurance. After everything checked out, they went back inside and began waking up the assigned passengers for each bus and escorted them out to their buses. The sleepy, groggy passengers, all carrying their duffle bags said their good-byes to one another and to Delores and her staff and thanked them for their help and kindness in their troubled lives. Once everyone was on board and checked off of lists, the four buses pulled out from the shelter; one to St. Louis, one to Chicago, one to St. Paul and one to Denver.

After the buses left; a moving van pulled up and a crew began loading all of the beds and bedding and all of the furniture, including all of the kitchen and dining room furniture and all of the office equipment and furniture. Delores and her staff then began loading a large van with all of their boxed up paperwork and all of the records of the shelters supporters and donators. When their van and the large van were loaded, they turned out the lights and locked the doors. They all climbed into their van and headed to an undisclosed location about thirty outside of San Antonio. The shelter had acquired the rental of an abandoned motel where they would set up operations of a new shelter.

At about six A.M. a SWAT, (Specialized Weapons and Tactics) team employed by the US Border Patrol arrived at the building. The US Border Patrol had been ordered by Washington to eliminate these refugee centers in the southwestern border states as part of the policy of President Trump to put an end to immigration from Mexico. The SWAT team broke down the front door of the now evacuated refugee shelter. But as the Border Patrol entered the building, they found nothing but an empty warehouse.

The four busloads of refugees were already about a hundred miles away, heading north, up I-35to their designated destinations, into the heartland of America. They would arrive, after several days travel at yet another refugee shelter. Here they will begin their journey to becoming productive U.S. citizens.

* * * * * *

Mike and Audrey return to their motel suite in Brainerd and call their insurance agent.

"I don't know if you are covered in the case of arson," He informs them, "I'll go ahead and submit it to our underwriter, but I just don't think you'll get the full value of your house. You know; I just talked to the Sheriff of Crow Wing County. Both he and the Fire Chief agree, it looks like someone is out to get you, maybe even kill you. If I were you, I'd disappear for a while."

"I agree with the insurance agent, Mike. Maybe we should just disappear for a while. I think we could use a little vacation after all we've been through this past year. I've been looking at ads and brochures on Hawaii. How about we go right now seeing as how we don't dare go back to Arizona again"

"Okay, Honey, I agree, "we do need to get away for a while and 'disappear' like the insurance guy said. And we do have the money, no doubt. But first we need to deal with rebuilding our lake house. Here's an idea; how about we rebuild, but then use the new house as just our summer home and buy a permanent house in the Twin Cities. We've certainly got enough money to have both."

"I agree, let's do both."

Mike finds a building contractor and hires him to rebuild their lake house. Next, he and

Audrey head to the cities and spend about a week looking at houses in the city. They find one that they really like in the St. Paul suburb of White Bear Lake. They sign the purchase agreement and close with a cash deal with money from their off-shore account. After again shopping for furniture, they book a flight and a condo on Maui for two weeks.

For now, at least, they don't tell any of their children about their new situation, about their house at Thunder Lake being torched by the unknown assailant. They are fearful that if the kids know, they could be forced into telling this person where they will now be living.

The snowbirds return home from Hawaii just before Thanksgiving, after two weeks of relaxing on Hawaii's warm beaches. They feel rejuvenated and ready to continue their battle with whomever was trying to destroy them.

"Let's have a big Thanksgiving dinner at our new house and invite all of our children," Audrey says.

"Sounds like a great idea. We've certainly got plenty of room now. This house is huge."

The Thanksgiving dinner is a huge success. All of the children and grandchildren are very happy to see them back in Minnesota, safe and sound, or so they believe. They are not told the whole story.

"So, what made you decide to move back to the city," son Chris asks?

"Well, we decided the lake house is just too remote. It's located too far up north and far from amenities, such as groceries, and other shopping, and medical facilities. As we are getting older we need to be closer to those facilities."

"Well it's so good to have you back in the city," Rachel says, "Now we can see you more often and look out for you as you get older."

"What about the lake house?" Richard asks.

"Well, we're keeping it for a while. It'll be our summer home and all you children are invited up in the summer, anytime you need to get away."

They do not disclose to the children yet, the very large sum of money they had acquired. They wanted to make sure that they had the issue of being followed and the destruction of the lake house resolved before they made any decision about disbursing any of the windfall to the children.

Heidi asks, "What made you decide to get such a large house? You've got five bedrooms, four bathrooms, and a lower level family room with a kitchenette."

"Well, it's not so much the room, it was just such a great buy we couldn't pass it up. So now we've got a ton of equity here to pass on to you kids when we pass on. And besides, now we have plenty of room for when all the grandkids and great grandkids come to sleep over."

"Whatever happened with that thing with the FBI questioning all of us last spring," Roger asks?

"We haven't heard anything more from them. Either – A; they think we were killed in that bridge accident, or – B; they caught up with those cartel guys with the drugs."

"Well, thank God that's over," Linda says, we were all worried sick about you. You two snowbirds need to settle down now that you have got this great house, and quit chasing all over the country. You're getting too old for all that excitement."

"Yah, Yah, whatever,' Audrey says, "We're not the 'settle down' types. Besides, once you stop having fun, then you really get old. We'll be back on the snowbird trail again soon. You can bet on it."

After the dinner was all cleaned up and a football game was watched, the kids and grandkids all left saying, "Thanks for the fabulous dinner, Mom, and, great house, Dad."

RETRIBUTION

After all the children left; Audrey said, "Come on Mike, we have to hurry. I've signed us up to volunteer at the Salvation Army's homeless and refugee centers in downtown St. Paul, They'll be serving their Thanksgiving dinners soon.. I have this friend of mine, Chris, who knows the director and he said he needs servers."

"Thanks for signing us up, Honcy, I think it's the least we can do as a small measure of payback for the blessings we have been afforded."

They hurried downtown and find a parking ramp near the Salvation Army Mission. However, they were told that they had enough volunteers at the mission. The head of the mission told them that they still needed servers at the refugee center, down on the riverfront. Mike and Audrey headed over there. Near downtown St. Paul in a riverfront building on Shepard Road, behind the old Schmidt Brewery, overlooking the

Mississippi River, the second through the fourth floors are occupied by a refugee center, sponsored by the Salvation Army. Mike and Audrey find that they were just beginning to serve dinner, so they scrubbed in and got their vinyl gloves on and joined the serving line.

On the fourth floor the Mendoza and Ramirez families were waiting their turn to be called down for their first Thanksgiving Dinner in the USA. They had arrived from the now shuttered San Antonio refugee center just three weeks ago and already the children were enrolled in school. Because they all spoke English, they were assigned to a Charter School in the Midway area of the Twin Cities, on the corner of Minnehaha and Como Avenues. They had already applied for 'green card' status and were attending citizenship classes.

"At school yesterday we learned that today is a very big important holiday in the US. Everyone celebrates by eating a very big meal and watching football games on TV," Madeline stated, "And we learned that the game of American football is kind of like soccer, only the ball isn't round and they mostly pick it up and run with it and only sometimes kick it."

"Then what's for dinner Momma?" little Antonio asks, "I'm getting very hungry."

"I'll answer that," Juanita says, "We learned about that just this week in our cooking class. The main meat is roasted turkey, which tastes kind of like chicken. The turkey is first stuffed with a mixture made up of dried bread cubes, onion, chopped apple or raisins, all moistened with drippings from cooking the turkeys gizzard, liver and neck which are all chopped intro the dressing and seasoned with a special poultry seasoning. Also there is mashed potatoes with gravy and another potato called sweet potato, garnished with marshmallow, followed by a vegetable of either squash or corn. For dessert everyone has a slice of a pie made from the pumpkin or a piece of apple or blueberry pie topped with whipped cream."

"Oh, my God, that sounds so delicious," Carlotta says, "but so much food. No wonder these Americans are all fat and overweight."

"We want to have some pumpkin pie," The twins, Jose and Christina exclaim together.

"Well, first you must eat your turkey and vegetables," Carlotta scolds.

A few minutes later they are called down to dinner. As they all sat down to dinner, a Thanksgiving prayer was said by everyone, many in their own native language, Spanish.

Later that evening, as Audrey and Mike were on their way home, Audrey says, "Well that was such a great experience, helping feed those refugees. We need to do that more often.

"I know, for many of them, this was their first Thanksgiving meal in the USA."

"Wasn't that a cute family with the little twins, and that little five year old; Antonio, I think the mother called him. He loaded up his plate with some of everything. He must have been very hungry. The other children just took select items. The mother must have her hands full with that brood, with no husband with them. Don't you wonder what the story is there? That whole family spoke English quite well. I wonder what that story is. That oldest daughter sure knew how to take charge of her younger siblings. She must be a big help to that single mom, and she is only a young teenager."

"I know, so many broken families trying to escape the tyranny in their homeland."

"Yeah, it's kind of like the story of all Americans. Immigrating to America, that's how every one of us came to be here. I hope we can help them in more ways as time allows."

The next day, Black Friday as it's come to be called, finds the Mendoza and Ramirez family back in their fourth floor apartment after a late breakfast in the cafeteria. By mid-morning, they all migrate down to the lounge on the second floor. The Thanksgiving day football games are over and it's cartoon time. As most of America heads to the malls for Black Friday bargains. the refugees stay put. Most don't know what Black Friday is. Even if they did, they couldn't participate. Most have not worked yet and earned American dollars to spend.

* * * * * *

Halfway across the continent, Las Vegas picked up the phone, Juan Carlos was on the line, calling from across the Twin Cities in the Minneapolis suburb of Maple Grove.

"Hey boss, I think I've got a lead on those drug thieves. They're having their lake house rebuilt. I talked to one of the workers. He said they have bought a new house here in the Twin Cities. Now I will be able to track them down and find where they live. At least they are closer and I won't have to keep running up to the north. I hate driving on these slippery roads. I hate all this snow and cold. It's snowing again today."

"Well, look at it this way; it's damn cold in the ground, in a coffin, which is where you'll be if you don't get that damn information soon. Bogota is running out of patience, hell, I'm running out of patience. So get the hell out there in the snow and get that damn information. We're not going to wait forever, you know."

* * * * * *

On Sunday morning, Mike picked up the Sunday paper. There, on the front page was the story of President Trump's order to close all the refugee centers in the border states and send all the refugees back to Mexico. The article went on to say that Trump wants to close the refugee centers in all the cities that have these 'safe harbors' for refugees. Mike shows the article to Audrey.

"Whatever will become of those refugees down at the refugee center in downtown St. Paul?" Audrey asks.

"I suppose the US Immigration Service will send them all back to Mexico."

"Can't we do something, Mike, we can't let that happen, especially to that cute little family that we saw at the Thanksgiving dinner. Hey, maybe we could house them here. Think about it. We have that huge basement with a kitchenette and everything."

"You know, Honey, I think you're right. We have the resources and the money to make a difference in those people's lives. Let's fight back against the tyranny in our own country;

against the Trump tyranny. How about you call that friend of yours and see if we can get that family out of that center before they are split up and sent back to Mexico, where they'll surely be murdered by the drug cartel."

"I could really use some help keeping up this big house of ours. That mother of the refugee family could work right here as our housekeeper. That way she could take care of the little one's right here and wouldn't need a sitter while she works."

"I'll check with the local elementary school and see if the school aged children can transfer to a school here in White Bear Lake."

"So let's get going on this. We don't have much time before the US Immigration Service closes that refugee center."

Audrey immediately calls that friend of a friend at the Riverside Refugee Center and explains their plan to take the refugee family into their home.

"Oh, that would be excellent. We've been working twenty-four-seven to get these families placed somewhere with sponsors, ever since we heard about Trump's plan to close all the safe harbor centers in all the cities. Why don't you and your husband come in for an interview right away. I have an opening tomorrow morning at seven."

Mike and Audrey spent the rest of the day shopping for furniture for their new residents; living room, kitchen, dining room, seven bed and dresser sets and of course a large screen TV.

The next morning on their way downtown to the Riverfront Refugee Center, they drove along mostly silent. Each one was deep in thought about their new big commitment and where it will lead them.

“I sure hope we’re doing the right thing here. This is a very big commitment,” Audrey says.

“Well, it sure seems like the right thing to do right now. Who knows about the future. Life, it seems is just one grand adventure with no guarantee of any expected outcome. But, you know. we’ve had our own children move back home from time to time, with their families. How can this be much different?”

The Riverfront Refugee Center was a very busy place on that snowy morning. When they arrived, dozens of the refugees were departing, some by bus, some by cars.

“Well,” Audrey says, “This makes me feel much better about sponsoring a family. All these people departing have obviously found sponsors.”

At the door, they ask to see the shelter director, Beverly Hansen. Her secretary had them fill out a sponsor qualification form, which was quickly reviewed by a placement review committee. After which they were welcomed in by the director, Ms. Hansen.

"Your application passed our review board. As you can see, we're in a hurry-up mode today to get all the refugees out of here that we can. The Immigration Service could come in and close us down at any moment, without any warning. I'll have to make this quick; just a brief history of this family: They are from Chihuahua, Mexico. They have endured horrific treatment and torture at the hands of the Medellin drug cartel. The four oldest children, the Mendoza's have had their parents killed in a drug deal gone bad. The oldest child, Juanita, who is just fifteen has been raped repeatedly by a cartel agent trying to get information about their parents. Carlotta, the mom and her husband had adopted the Mendoza's. The cartel agent came into their home and murdered her husband; shot him in the head, right in front of her and the children. He then beat and raped Juanita again, and as he was leaving, he threatened to come back and rape and kill them all if they didn't tell him what happened to the missing drugs from that bad drug deal. That's why they left Mexico. Carlotta had a friend who got them across the border into El Paso and on to the refugee center in San Antonio. But, when Trump's orders came down to close all the refugee centers in border states, they were transferred here to St. Paul.

You will get a copy of this report when you leave here. All of our records are being transferred to a secret location and will be destroyed after seven years.

Carlotta already has a Green Card. She and all of the children can speak English. They have no possessions except a few clothing items and what they are wearing. They are packed and ready to go, if you are willing to sign for them. We have a van ready to take them to your house right away. A Social Worker from the Salvation Army will visit them monthly to see how they are adjusting to life in the US. If you have any further questions or problems, you can call our District Office and they will try to help out. If there are no further questions and you feel like you are ready for this responsibility, please just sign this acceptance form."

Mike and Audrey both sign the form as a van pulls up in the snow outside and inside the Mendoza and Ramirez gather in the lounge and are introduced to their sponsors.

"Oh, I remember you," Carlotta said, "You two were serving at the Thanksgiving dinner."

"Yes, we were," Audrey said, "and we thought you and all your children would be someone we'd like to sponsor and invite to come and live with us. We have a very large house with plenty of room for all of you."

"Well, why don't you all get loaded into the van and follow us to our house. We'll talk more when we get there."

Carlotta and the children load into the van as the snow continues to fall, and the driver follows Mike and Audrey to their house in White Bear Lake.

"Golly, the snow is so pretty, falling from the sky," Madeline comments, "It's like tiny pieces of the clouds floating down to earth."

"I know," Antonio adds, "I can't wait to play in it. Is it cold, Mom?"

"Yes it is, Dear, very cold to touch. That's why they gave us those mittens to wear."

"I can't wait to get to our house," Juan says, "Do you think it will be nice?"

"I'm sure it will be. Most U.S. homes are very nice, and those people who own the house seem very nice."

"I can't wait to have my own bed to sleep in," Juanita says, "And to start school in our new school, and make some new friends."

They arrive at the house and Mike and Audrey guide them down stairs to their new apartment, after shutting off the alarm system.

"Oh, my God," Carlotta exclaims, "This place is so huge. Is this all for us?"

"Yes," Audrey explains, "This is your apartment. There are three bedrooms; one for you and one for the girls and one for the boys."

"Mom, look," Madeline exclaims, "These bedrooms are huge and we each have our own bed. These dressers are beautiful, but how will we ever fill them up?"

"Well, I suspect we have a lot of shopping to do," Audrey says.

"Oh, my gosh," Juanita yells from the living room, "Would you look at the size of this television. It's like a movie theater."

"Look, over here," Juan exclaims from near the dining room, "Look at this huge glass wall, or whatever. What is this? Is it a window or is it a door of some kind? I've never seen anything like this before."

"It's called a patio door, Juan. I've seen pictures of these in American magazines."

"How does it open?"

"I don't really know. We'll have to ask someone."

Mike and Audrey were standing with Carlotta in the kitchen, explaining to her how all the appliances worked.

"Mister Mike,“ Juan called, "Could you show how this patio door works."

"Okay, sure," Mike replied, "But first I have to explain how the security system in this house works. Everyone gather around over here by the kitchen cupboards. See this small door here on the wall next to the cupboard. Behind this door is the control panel for the security alarm system. There is also one upstairs in the hall near the top of the stairs. Whenever we leave the house, we push this red button marked 'SET'. That will turn on the alarm system. You then have thirty seconds to open the door, leave and close the door. After that, the system is set. In other words, if there is a break-in through any door or window, a very loud alarm will sound. At the same time, the system will be calling the police call center. A few seconds after that, the house phone will ring. I'll show you where that phone is kept in a minute. You must immediately answer the phone and enter the alarm code. I'll give you the code when I'm through explaining how the system works. If you enter the exact code, nothing will happen and you just push the system re-set button. If, however, someone has broken into the house, either don't answer that call, or if you are being forced to answer the call, then; enter the wrong code and a police car will be sent out to the house immediately."

When you first come into the house, you will hear a beeping sound. Again you have thirty seconds to turn off the alarm system by entering the alarm code and then pushing the OFF button.

Our house has alarm sensors on all the windows and doors, this includes the patio doors and garage door. If any one of these sensors is interrupted, the system alarm will sound and activate the auto call to the police call center.

We normally leave the system off during the day when we are home and turn it on a night or when we leave. But if you are home alone, even during the day, you can turn it on to feel more secure. All of the doors, including the two patio doors, up and down have a key pad locking system. So instead of a key, you just enter the code into the keypad to unlock the door. That code is the same as the alarm system code.

Okay, listen up everybody; the code is: 38642. Memorize that code and do not tell anyone or write it down anywhere. The police phone is kept in the cupboard above the kitchen stove. One is down here and one upstairs.

Now we'll practice using the system. You'll each take a turn; setting the alarm, using the SET button and going out through the door and closing it. Then entering the code into the door keypad, open the door and hear the alarm beeping. Run to the control panel and enter the code again and push the OFF button. We'll practice it until we feel comfortable doing it."

Carlotta and the Mendoza children practiced it several times until they were sure they could do it.

"It's a bit scary at first," Juanita says, "But I feel sure that I can do it. How about you Madeline?"

"Well, we've never done anything like this before, but I'm, sure we all can do it now."

"Okay, good," Mike says, "because we need to go out and get some groceries. Carlotta will come with Audrey and I and learn how to shop for groceries in America using the dollar system. Juanita, you stay with the rest of the children. You can all watch TV while we're out. We will set the alarm as we leave. So no one is to go outside until we get back. When we return with the groceries, we'll have lunch, then we'll take you, Juanita and the older children out shopping for some new clothes.

Later, when Audrey, Mike and the Mendoza children get home from the first of many shopping trips, Carlotta had fixed a huge dinner of excellent Mexican cuisine. She invited them to stay. Audrey told her that she doesn't need to cook for Mike and herself.

"We will cook for ourselves, upstairs. Your job for us will be to do the cleaning, dusting, bed making and the laundry. I'll help you get started. Maybe you can help cook if we have friends or relatives over for dinner, like during the holidays. We have a very large family."

After dinner, the dishes are cleared by Juan and Madeline and loaded into the dishwasher.

"This machine is like magic," Madeline states.

"I know," says Juan, "I've never seen one of these things before. We just put the dishes in there, add the special soap, close it up, push the start button and later you open it and the dishes are ready to put away, just like magic."

"There are so many magical things in our new home. I love the bathroom most of all. I love taking a bath in the shower instead of that old tin tub we had in LaJunta, in our first house, before our Mom and Dad went away." as she started to become teary-eyed.

"I know, I know," Juan consoles her and changes the subject back to the bathroom, I love the running water here. You just turn a faucet and you get hot or cold water, instead of bringing in water by carrying buckets from the town pump and heating it on the kitchen stove."

"I love using the toilet and the water just swooshes everything away; instead of using that stinky old outhouse."

Mike overhears them talking and decides to show them where all the 'magic' happens. He leads them to the utility room, located behind the stairs. "That big round thing over there is where the water is heated. It has a gas burner in the base of it which comes on as needed based on the temperature of the water. The water comes into the house up through the floor through that pipe over in the corner from a large pipe out under the street that everyone shares. That big boxy looking metal thing is the furnace. Those metal tubes sticking out of it. carry the cold air in from each room and the heated air is returned by a large fan through another tube back to each room."

"Wow," Madeline says, "See Juan, I told you. This house is just full of magical things. I just love magical things."

"Okay children," Carlotta says, "Let's watch one more show on the TV and then it's off to bed. We've had a very busy day in our new home. Mr. and Mrs. Felder, thank you so, so much for sponsoring us and sharing your beautiful house with us. How can we ever repay you.? We will be forever grateful to you."

"Well, you are all very welcome," Audrey says, "We're happy to have you here. The one way you can show your appreciation is by becoming productive citizens in this, your new country."

After the TV show and all the children are into their beds and asleep; Audrey asks Carlotta. “How did the Mendoza children lose their parents?”

“Oh, I was afraid you’d ask that sooner or later. I don’t have all the facts. Nobody really does, I guess. All I know is that their parents were drug runners for the drug cartels. They had their own plane and flew drugs into the US. Last year at Christmas, they were on a drug run and went missing, somewhere in the US. Nobody knows where they went. Not even the Mendellin cartel, apparently. That’s why the cartel agent came to our house a short time after we adopted the children and started to brutally question us all. They thought we might know something. He raped Juanita repeatedly and shot and killed my husband, Antonio right in front of me and the children. That man is the devil.”

“Oh, We’re so sorry,” Audrey said, “Your family has been through so much.”

“Well, I do hope you all will be safe here,” Mike said.

“Thank you for understanding and listening to our story. I’ve wanted to get this off my chest all day.”

“Well, your family has been incredibly brave through that horrible nightmare ordeal.

We'll do everything we can to keep you safe from the likes of any more cartel brutality."

"Well, I don't know about you," Audrey says, "But I'm exhausted. It's been a really long day for everyone. Come on Mike, lets head upstairs to our half of the house and let Carlotta get some sleep. I'll bet she's totally exhausted also."

"Yes," Mike agreed, "Tomorrow will be quite busy as well. We'll get the school children started in their new school, and do some more shopping as well. We will leave the door at the top of the stairs always unlocked, so if there's anything you need, or questions, feel free to come up anytime."

Mike and Audrey head upstairs and get ready for bed.

"Mike, this is incredible," Audrey begins, after they are in bed, "If what Carlotta said is true, and the report by the shelter is true, - - - then this is the family of the drug runners whose plane wreckage we found in that canyon and took out all of that money in that backpack. Oh, my God, Mike,- - - what do we do now?"

"This changes everything, Honey. That money, at least some of it should really go to that family. Here's what I think we should do: take some of the money that's in the Edward Jones investment account and convert it over to trust accounts for each of the Mendoza children. What do you think?"

"That sounds great. How about half of it. That will still leave us one million in Edward Jones, plus the money in that off-shore account.

The next day Mike visited an Edward Jones office and set up the trust accounts for the four Mendoza children. He put two hundred and fifty thousand dollars into each trust

THE ROAD TO PERDITION

The Mendoza children; Juanita, Juan, Madeline and Antonio were enrolled in the White Bear Elementary School. The two Ramirez twins; Jose and Christina were allowed to play in the snowy back yard on the warmer days of early December while the school kids were at school. The back yard was fenced in, so they could play safely. They created snowmen and built a snow fort. When the school kids came home from school, they would join in the fun in the fresh snow. These idyllic days passed all too quickly. As more fresh snow fell, the children took each new snow and molded it into more snow people. Soon they had a replica of each family member.

By mid-December, as the days grew shorter and shorter, the temperature kept sliding, like a toboggan racing down a steep hill. It was too cold now for the little ones to play outside.

Even with their mittens, their fingers would tingle and hurt. The bigger children also found that the colder snow would not stick into the shapes they might want to create. Everyone was now confined to the inside world. Homework, of course, occupied the evening hours for the school children. For the little twins, of course, there was more time spent in front of the TV. The sun seemed less and less effective at chasing away the bitter cold of the heart of winter.

Carlotta approached Audrey as she was doing her daily chores upstairs.

"What is happening to our temperature," she asked, "I checked the outside thermometer and it read zero. How much colder does it get here in Minnesota?"

"Well, it can get a lot colder. Sometimes it gets as low as twenty, even thirty below zero."

"How does everyone survive in those temperatures?"

"One of the secrets is to spend as little time as possible outside. That's why you will see people hurrying through the snow to get back inside."

On one cold mid-December morning after a fresh snowfall of several inches, as the school children were leaving to catch their bus and were climbing the steps up from their lower level, up to the sidewalk that went around the front of the house they found fresh footprints on the steps and in the back yard. They immediately told their mom about the footprints in the fresh snow. She told the children to stay inside while she checked them out. They were not footprints from any of the children. They were large adult sized footprints in the fresh snow. Probably made sometime during the night right after the fresh snowfall. Carlotta rushed back inside and locked the door and set the alarm system. She informed the children that they would not be going to school today. She told them to close all the curtains and blinds and stay away from the door and windows. She ran upstairs and found Audrey and Mike just finishing breakfast.

"There's somebody's footprints in the fresh snow in the backyard," she exclaimed excitedly and out of breath from running up the stairs, "I hope it's not someone from I.C.E.(Immigration and Customs Enforcement), coming to take my children away and force us all to go back to Mexico."

"Well, Carlotta, don't go panicking just yet. Good thing we have the security system."

Mike put on his hat, coat and boots and went out to check out the footprints. Sure enough, the footprints looked like they came around the backyard fence and through the gate at the top of the steps and down into the backyard.

The footprints shuffled around by the patio door, probably checking to see if it was locked. The prints then went over to the living room, dining room and bedroom windows with the same shuffling around.

Mike went back inside and called the police and reported it. A little while later an officer came by the house. He checked the footprints in the backyard snow and came back and confirmed to Mike and Audrey that it was indeed someone casing the house. He told them to keep the security system on at all times, and that he would have a patrol car drive by the house frequently at night. After he left, Mike went downstairs and told Carlotta what the officer had said, that it was probably a burglar. and that he would drive the kids to school and pick them up after and that they were not to take the bus until the issue was resolved.

Later, Audrey suggested that maybe he should get a gun for protection.

"No, no," He replied, "You know how I feel about having a gun. You're about ten times more likely to get yourself shot. If you confront someone with a gun, he will shoot first, every time. The perpetrator who is engaged in a crime with a gun is already convinced he can shoot anyone approaching him and he will, because he has nothing to lose. Where as, you or I will approach with caution and hesitation and that second of hesitation will get you shot first. It's all about opposite mind-sets. I hate guns, even though I have hunting rifles at the lake house. Hunting an animal is quite different than shooting another human being, believe me."

There were times, however, when he might have thought to change his philosophy. On several trips to school and back with the kids, he was almost certain that the same car was following him.

Almost a week went by. Everyone remained very tense and watchfully suspicious of anything out of the ordinary. Mike and Audrey finished their Christmas shopping. Sometimes Carlotta would accompany them. They gave her an agreed amount of money to shop with for the children, but only after she insisted it be an advance on her salary. The children were becoming irritable because they were not allowed to go out, except to school.

"It's like we're prisoners in this house," Juanita and Juan complained. 'We can't even see our friends after school. I don't see why we can't go shopping for Christmas. I still have some of the money that our parents left for us."

"I'm sorry, but no, Honey, It's just too dangerous out there right now."

Carlotta tried to explain that she thought that those tracks in the back could be from I.C.E, and they could force them to go back to Mexico.

"Why can't we just get a policeman to accompany us," Madeline pleaded.

"Because, that's not his job. They only patrol our house at night."

Carlotta relayed her concerns to Mike and Audrey.

You know," Mike said, "I just got a call from our contractor up at the lake. He said they have finished the re-build of our lake house. How about we head up there for the holidays? I've been wanting to check it out anyway before we pay him."

"Okay," Audrey says, "But first we wanted to have a Christmas party here for the kids and grandkids. They all want to meet our new residents. I've already sent out invitations."

Decorating the house began in earnest. This seemed to get everyone in a better mood, albeit a bit of trepidation about the approaching anniversary of that ill-fated Christmas Eve when their parents never came home and disappeared forever.

Saturday, a week before Christmas, the house was ready. All of Audrey and Mike's children and grandchildren and greatgrandchildren arrived by six and were introduced to the new members of their family

A huge buffet dinner was served. After the dessert was served and more drinks were pored, gifts were exchanged and all of the younger children checked out their new toys and played with the new members of their family. Young Charles thought Antonio was a really cool dude. Sam thought Madeline was just super cute. Little Katie and her sister Josephine played together with the twins, Jose and Christine for hours. The girls all got new Barbie dolls. Jose got LEGOs and built a house for the Barbie's. After several hours of playing together, Jose and Christina approached Audrey and Mike.

"Can we start calling you Grandma and Grandpa like Katie and Josephine do? Please, please, we don't have any of our own, you know. the drug people made them all dead, just like our Mama and Papa."

Antonio and Madeline overheard the conversation and came over.

"Us too, please," they both said.

They were followed by Juan and Juanita.

"I hope we're not too old to also call you Grandma and Grandpa."

"Oh, my darlings, no one will ever be too old for that. We would be honored and thrilled to be called Grandma and Grandpa by all of you."

You know, that now makes us all one wonderful family."

With that, everyone starting clapping and cheering, and the adults all raised their glasses in a toast. The expanded family now numbered about thirty seven. Cars were jammed into the driveway and along the street. As Mike answered the door for the last arrivals, he glanced out to the street. There was a car parked in with the rest of the guest's cars on the street that he recognized as the one that he thought he saw following him to school and back with the kids.

* * * * * *

There were two people sitting in that car, Juan Carlos and his co-worker friend from El Paso, Vasquez the butcher.

"So when do I get to have my fun with these people that we followed around all week in this beastly cold?"

"Probably not tonight, They'll be partying half the night with all those people. How about we hit them tomorrow?"

"No, I don't work on Sunday. That's the Lords day."

"Okay, how about we get them after midnight tomorrow?"

"That'll be better. Let's us just get it done and get the hell out of this frozen country. The rest of these crazy people can get back to living like friggin Eskimos. Now let's get ourselves back to our hotel where it's warm. I hate all this snow and cold up here in the north."

* * * * * *

After midnight, after everyone left. Mike set the security system, but no one went to bed yet. They all began packing for the trip up to the lake house at Thunder Lake.

"Pack all of your warm winter clothes," Carlotta told the children, "Pack wool socks and those 'long-johns' as they call them in this north country. Audrey told me that we'll be spending a lot of time outside at the lake house."

"Does the water in the lake freeze solid?" Antonio asked his mom.

"Well, I suspect it freezes some. We'll just have to wait and see."

By two A.M. they had the van loaded with clothes, toys and some of the Christmas decorations from the house.

"Okay," Carlotta announced to the children after everything was loaded into the van, "We have a couple of hours before we have to leave so everyone get to bed and get to sleep. I'll wake you when it's time."

Upstairs, Mike set their alarm for five A.M.

"I want to get on the road before daylight. It'll be easier to see if there's headlights from anyone following us."

At five A.M., Mike and Audrey carefully checked the perimeter of their house and the street out front. No one was around. Audrey went downstairs and woke Carlotta and she got all the children up and dressed, and loaded into the van. Audrey set the alarm system and Mike carefully and quietly backed the van out of the garage and they left for the lake.

At six thirty they stopped at a McDonalds in the town of Anoka. They all ate egg Mc Muffins. A light snow began falling as they got back on the road again, back on Highway 10 and headed north. Mike had not seen any headlights following them. At eight o'clock they stopped for gas and 'potty' at an S.A. station in the town of Brainerd

"Okay, let's finish up our Christmas shopping as long as we're right here at this shopping strip," Audrey said, "we should be safe here, away from the city."

"Oh, thank God for that," Juanita remarked, "At long last we get to do our Christmas shopping."

The snow continued to fall, heavier than ever as they shopped at Target, Kohls, Herberger and Wal Mart. While they took a break at a Starbucks, Mike shopped at Fleet Farm for some more outdoor gear, snowmobile gear and fishing supplies. After a stop at Cub Foods for groceries the van was packed to the roof. They all crammed in like sardines. One more hour and they arrived at the Thunder lake house. Mike went in first and turned off the alarm. Audrey followed after telling the rest to wait a minute in the van. They did a walk-through to check out all the features of the rebuild.

"This looks good to me," Audrey said, "They did a great job here, and the modifications are all as we asked for,"

"Okay, I'll write a check to the builder when he stops by later."

When Carlotta and the children came in they were given a tour of the house and each one was assigned a bedroom. The children brought in their bags and unpacked, then did more exploring on their own. Mike, meantime got a roaring fire going in the fireplace.

“Oh, this is so cozy and warm,” Carlotta remarked.

What’s that cute little house off of the side of the deck?” Juanita asked.

That’s our hot tub room,” Audrey replied, “Later I’ll show you how to use it.”

“Where’s the lake?” Little Antonio asked as he came from the deck.

“It’s down at the bottom of the hill,” Mike replied, “It’s that big flat looking area all covered with ice and snow.”

“Is it frozen solid?” he asked for the second time.

“No, no, just the surface, about two feet down. The water is quite deep out there, about twenty or thirty feet deep. That’s deeper than this house.

“Wow, that’s a lot of water, and ice too.”

“Maybe tomorrow we’ll go down and walk out on the lake ice and go ice fishing.”

“Oh, I don’t know, that sounds scary, walking on the lake.”

“It’ll be okay, you’ll see.”

“Okay everyone,” Mike said, “If you’ve checked out the whole house, there’s something I want to show you that you probably missed.”

He led them down to the basement. There, hidden within the paneling, was a secret door. He slid the paneling aside and exposed a steel clad door. Mike punched in the code. "This is the same code as the house code, which is the same as the city house code."

They all entered the secret room behind the furnace. The room was equipped with furniture, bunks along the wall, a bathroom, and food and water for a long stay if needed.

"This is our safe room," he explained, "If anyone starts to break into the house, you will all run down to this room and close and lock the door. The room is fire proof. There is a camera system throughout the house and on the outside, on the deck and down the driveway. You can view what the cameras see on these monitors here on the wall."

He turned on one of the monitors to demonstrate it. On the monitor they could see Audrey working in the kitchen.

"Also, over here on the table is an emergency satellite phone that's on a continuous charger, so you can call out for help. The entire system is run on standby batteries, that means, that even if the house power is out, the camera system will work and you will have lights here in this room."

"Wow," Carlotta said, "Hopefully we'll never need it. But it's comforting to know that it's here."

"Okay, everybody, let's go back upstairs and spend the rest of the day decorating this house." While Audrey, Carlotta and the girls and the twins began decorating, Mike and the boys went out into the garage where he started up one of the snowmobiles. He hitched up a cutter behind it and the three woodsmen went off down the snowmobile trail a short distance and found a nice sized Christmas. tree. Mike showed Juan and Antonio how to saw down the tree. They loaded it into the cutter and headed back and attached the base to the tree and brought it into the house and set it up.

"Look Mom," Antonio said, "Juan and I, we're real lumberjacks. We cut down this tree.

"Well, I'm real proud of you boys, It's a beautiful tree."

The children all worked together decorating it. Meanwhile, Carlotta and Audrey began work on a large pot of Carlotta's great Mexican chili. By suppertime, the tree was decorated and the chili was ready. Everyone ate heartily after a day of some outdoor activity and getting to know their new house in the woods, on the lake.

"Tomorrow," Mike said, "We'll do some more snowmobiling and maybe try our luck at ice fishing."

The family settled down at the dining room table after Mike and the boys cleared the dishes and loaded the dishwasher. They played cards, Gin Rummy, then some board games with the little twins; Chutes and Ladders and The Game of Life. By eight o'clock, everyone was ready for bed. It had been a very long day; up at five A.M. and the two hundred mile trip up north to the cabin on Thunder Lake, Christmas shopping along the way. Putting up the tree and decorating the house and the tree.

Everyone was asleep within minutes of hitting the pillows.

* * * * * *

Two hundred miles south of Thunder Lake at five minutes after midnight, a car pulled into the driveway at 130802 Primrose Lane in White Bear Lake.

"Well Vasquez, it's Monday, let's go get that kid and the old couple and make them talk this time."

"Wait a minute Juan, let's make sure they're home first. I don't see any fresh tracks in the snow and there's no lights on. Usually they leave a security light on. We better check it out before we break in. After we trip the alarm, we only have a few minutes before the cops arrive."

The two cartel hit men got out and walked around the house, through the gate and down into the back yard. They began looking into the bedroom windows. Juan shined his flashlight through the gap between the curtains.

"There's nobody in there Vasquez whispers. The beds are all made up, but no kids in them. There's nobody home, Juan. They've slipped away somewhere."

"Maybe we can ask the neighbors where they went. We'll have to come back in the morning and ask around."

Later in the morning, they returned and caught one of the neighbors just leaving for work.

"Do you happen to know where Mike and Audrey went? We were supposed to meet with them this morning."

"Oh, they left on Sunday, They said they were going to fly down to Florida for a few days at Disney World with all the kids. I think they said they wanted to be back for Christmas. So maybe tomorrow."

"Well not much we can do here," Juan said, as they got back into their car, "We'll just have come back tomorrow night again. Let's go back to the hotel. Maybe the bar is open. It's never too early to start drinking."

* * * * * *

Up north, at Thunder Lake, Audrey, Mike and Carlotta were up and making breakfast for the gang. A short time later, the children were up.

"What are we going to do today?" asked Juan, "Can we do some more snowmobiling? That was so fun yesterday, getting the Christmas tree in."

"Can I learn to drive a snowmobile," Madeline asked, Please, please, Grandpa? I think that would be so fun. How about you Juanita?"

"Well, I think I already know how to drive. I've read up on it in a magazine," said Juanita, trying to be the ever big sister.

"Can I drive too?" Antonio says.

"You'll all get a chance to drive and ride along," Audrey promised, "Carlotta and I might just go for a ride as well, and Christina and Jose can ride along also, in the cutter."

After everyone had their breakfast of blueberry pancakes, scrambled eggs Ranchos Huevos and smoked sausages, the children all rushed off to get dressed.

"Hold on, just a minute," Carlotta yelled after them, "There's dishes to do. Grandma and I worked hard to make this hardy breakfast, but you get to do the dishes. Remember, work before play."

Mike supervised and pitched in as the kids did the clean-up and loaded the dishwasher.

"Okay," Mike said when dishes were done, "It looks like Grandpa's snowmobile driving school is now in session. The first thing we'll learn today is how to dress."

With that he went to the garage and got a huge sack of helmets that he had bought at the Fleet Farm store, along with face masks, bibs, goggles and very warm gloves for everyone. The children all found their sizes that fit and got everything on.

"Wow, we look like astronauts," commented Madeline.

"Or outer space aliens," Antonio said.

When they were all properly suited up, Mike pulled the four snowmobiles out of the garage. They were of varying sizes and power to match the ages of the children. A light snow was beginning to fall.

"Okay," Mike said after he explained how to start the machines and handle the throttle and brakes, "I will take one of you at a time. You will follow me and do what I do. We'll take a short run down Thunder Lake Road, out to the highway and back. We'll do this several times until everyone is comfortable handling their snowmobile. Then we'll go together on a nice long ride."

While each one was out on their training runs, Audrey got several toboggans out and showed the other kids where to slide down the hill to the lake. After a couple of hours of lessons, they were ready for a longer trail ride.
Mike hitched up the cutter to his big machine for the twins and led them all down Thunder Lake Road and across highway six into the state forest recreation area where there were about twenty miles of trails. The kids all took turns driving for a while. By noon they were ready to head back to the cabin for lunch. While they ate, Audrey and Carlotta took their turn on the snowmobiles. The snow was coming down heaver now. About two inches were already on the ground by the time Audrey and Carlotta got back and put the snowmobiles back in the garage.

THE DEVIL CLAIMS HIS DUE

Two hundred miles south of Thunder Lake, at 13082 Primrose Lane in White Bear Lake, at about five A.M. a car was parked about a half a block down the street.

"I don't see why we can't just break in now and wait for them inside."

"Because, you numbskull, if we break in, the alarm system will call the cops."

"Oh, I didn't know that. I just want to get inside, out of this cold."

The two cartel executioners continued waiting in their car with the motor running for about six more hours, until about noon.

"Ya know, I don't think they're coming home today."

"I thought you said that the neighbor said they were coming home for Christmas."

"I'm beginning to think that he lied to us. I'm beginning to think that they never went to

Disney World at all. I'll bet they went back up north to that lake place."

The two cartel agents took off. They filled up with gas and got a McDonalds for lunch then headed up Highway 10 toward Thunder Lake.

* * * * * *

At Thunder Lake, meanwhile, the Felder family had just finished their breakfast and were ready for more adventure.

"How about we try our luck at ice fishing," Grandpa Mike suggested."

"I don't know how to ice fish, but it sounds like fun," Juan said, "Let's try it."

"If everyone else goes out on the ice, I guess I'll go too," Antonio said with trepidation in his voice.

Mike went out to the garage and got the fishing gear. He gave each of them a bucket with a padded seat on top to sit on, out on the ice. Inside each bucket was the ice fishing tackle. He picked up the power ice auger and his bucket and led the procession of ice fishers down onto the lake and out onto the ice. They all walked out onto the ice for about thirty feet from shore.

"The water should be about ten or twelve feet deep here," he said.

"Wow," Juanita exclaimed, "It's like we're walking on water,"

"That's right," Audrey said, "but very hard water. When the water freezes, the ice floats on top of the water."

"Why is that?" Juan questioned.

"It's because water is made up of two gasses, hydrogen and oxygen. During the freezing process, the oxygen molecules which are lighter than the water, are trapped inside. This makes the ice lighter than the water beneath it and so it floats on top of the water."

Mike started up the ice auger and soon had nine holes drilled through the two feet of ice. He and Audrey showed Carlotta and the children how to bait their hooks. A short fishing pole and reel is used; only about two feet long. The fish line is strung out the tip of the rod. At the end of the line, the bait, called the jig is attached. The jig is a weighted lure with a hook surrounded by some feather-like material. A meal worm, or sometimes a minnow is put on the hook. It is lowered into the hole in the ice, down to near the bottom of the lake. The rod is then jerked slightly up and down in short movements, thus causing the lure to appear life-like to the fish.

Soon everyone was baited up and lines and lures into the holes.

It wasn't long before Antonio began shouting, "something is tugging on my line."

"Pull up quickly on your pole and begin winding the line in," Mike said, as he came over to help, "That's it, now pull your fish up and out through the hole."

In a minute there was a pan fish called a Crappie flipping around on top of the ice. Everyone came over to see it as Mike took it off of the hook and dropped it into a bucket. They all hurried back over to their jigs and soon they too were pulling fish out through the ice. After about an hour everyone had caught at least one, even the little twins, Jose and Christina caught one, some caught more. When they had a dozen fish in the bucket, Mike said it was time to quit for the day. There were 'Aw's from everyone,

"We have enough for a meal," Mike said, "We can come back out tomorrow and catch some more."

They all packed up their gear and trudged back up to the cabin. The snow was coming now, heaver that ever, and the temperature was plunging. The children were wet and cold. When they got their winter clothes off, Audrey asked them if they wanted to get into the hot tub to warm up. The kids and Carlotta got into their swimsuits and Audrey led them out to the hot tub hut where they eagerly climbed into the nice warm bubbly water. They all settled down into the warm bubbling water; while outside, a blizzard was beginning. Snow was coming down heavier than ever and the wind was howling and piling the snow into ever deepening drifts.

"Aah, this is like a little bit of heaven," Carlotta said.

"The bubbles tickle me all over," little Christina said.

While they were hot-tubbing , Mike cleaned their catch of fish and got them ready to go into the frypan for supper. After twenty minutes in the hot tub, followed by a fresh fish dinner, Mike announced that the Midnight Mass had been moved up to eight P.M. due to the blizzard. They all hurried and get dressed and loaded into the van. The snow was piling up to half a foot deep already and the north wind was howling. The twelve mile drive into town was treacherous. Half way there, they see flashing red lights up ahead. As they cross the bridge over a narrow arm of Roosevelt Lake they saw a car with a crunched front end being towed away from the bridge's guardrail where it apparently skidded in the snow. As they crept on by, out of the corner of his eye, Mike thinks the car looks vaguely familiar. They carefully made their way to the church of Saint Emily in the town of Emily. The Christmas Mass was short because of the storm. All the familiar Christmas hymns were sung by the small congregation.

As they make their way carefully back to their lake house cabin, they noticed that the tow truck and crunched car were gone from the bridge, probably towed to a garage in town.

* * * * * *

At that garage; Emily Auto Repair, Juan Carlos and his partner, Vasquez were seated in the garage waiting room.

"You know Juan, you don't drive so good."

"What the hell you talkin about? I got us safely this far in this blinding blizzard, didn't I? I hate this damn country so bad, It's nothing but snow, snow, snow. Just ice and snow everywhere, and it's always so damn cold. It's no wonder everybody that can, gets the hell out of here in the winter."

"Well, let's just get our job done and get the hell out of here. It looks like they have our car ready to run again."

They got into their car and crept slowly north again towards Thunder Lake. To their luck, a snowplow had made a single pass down the middle of highway 6. No plow however on Thunder Lake Road, but they follow the tire ruts of the Felder van. Snow is still coming down heavily and the howling wind is still piling it into deep drifts. It's almost midnight when they pull up just outside the driveway to wait, because lights are still on inside the cabin.

* * * * * *

Inside the cabin, the family is still in front of the TV. After returning from church, they all gathered in front of the TV to watch the movie; 'How the Grinch Stole Christmas'. Their gifts had been placed under the tree and the little one's were anxiously awaiting Santa. Juanita, Juan, Madeline and Antonio were all thinking to themselves; "What a difference this Christmas is from a year ago."

After the movie finished and the fire died down in the fireplace; a very tired family all crawled into bed. They were all asleep within minutes.

* * * * * *

Outside, on the road, the Grinch, the Devil himself, and his murderous partner observed through the blowing snow, the lights going out in the lake house and began discussing their fiendish strategy.

"Okay," Juan said, "Here's what we need to do; first we put on these ski masks. I'm certain the place is loaded with cameras, just like their house in the city. We have to act fast before their security system calls the cops. We'll cut the power to the house at the meter box on the outside wall next to the garage door, but the security system is probably on a battery backup system. So be prepared for a deafening loud screeching alarm. That's why I brought these sound suppressing ear muffs. We'll go in through the garage service door and then into the house. We'll head right upstairs. The old couples bedroom is on the left at the top of the stairs. We'll force them to get dressed then handcuff them, and you lead them out to the car and lock them in. Then hurry back in to help find that oldest girl. We'll get her dressed as well and out to the car and get the hell out before the cops get there."

"Why are we getting them dressed. We're going to kill them anyway, right after they tell us where the drugs and money are."

"Well, dumbass, we don't want them freezing to death before they talk."

They waited another half hour to make sure everyone was asleep. They pulled on their ski masks and ear muffs and Juan slowly and quietly pulled the car into the driveway with the lights off and backed up to the garage service door. First they clipped the seal on the electric box and meter next to the door. They flipped the main breaker and the yard and other security lights went dark and the power to the house went dead. Juan broke the glass panel in the garage service door. The alarm system immediately began to scream.

* * * * * *

In the downstairs bedroom, Carlotta woke up immediately and threw on a bathrobe and ran into the adjoining bedroom where the twins, Jose and Christina were also awake. The house was black dark and the alarm is deafening. The twins began to cry. Carlotta took one of them by the hand and ordered the others to also hold hands. The two boys, Juan and Antonio who were sleeping in bunk beds in the same bedroom join the twins as Carlotta led them town the hall in the blackness, to the basement stairs. Meantime Juanita joined them after feeling her way down from the upstairs. She don't realize that her sister, Madeline, a sound sleeper was not yet awake. With the alarm screaming and in the blackness, they carefully proceeded down, holding hands and the railing. Carlotta led them around back of the furnace where she slid the panel aside and found the Keypad lit up. She keyed in the code and they all entered the safe room and she closed the door behind them and turned on the light.

Upstairs, Mike and Audrey were slower to awake. Mike jumped out of bed and started to run for the door, yelling for Audrey to follow.

"Com'on Honey, hurry, let's get down to the safe room."

Just as they reached the door, the two intruders came around the door from the hall with flashlights blazing and pushed them back onto the bed. With the flashlights glaring in their faces, Juan yelled at them as he pointed his gun at them.

"Hurry up and get your damn clothes on, right now dammit.. You're coming with us. come ,on get to it or I'll shoot ya right here."

As the couple start to get dressed, Juan goes back out into the hall yelling, "I'll get the other one." ,leaving Vasquez to guard Mike and Audrey. In the other bedroom, Madeline woke up and ran for the door just as Juan came in shining his flashlight in her face, but in the limited light, Juan thought she is Juanita and ordered her to get dressed. Meanwhile across the hall, Mike and Audrey are dressed and Vasquez ordered them out to the stairs where he pointed his flashlight down the stairs for them as he followed with his gun pointed at them. In the other bedroom, Madeline is dressed and Juan ordered her out to the stairs and down. In the lower hall they were forced down the hall to the hall closet and all three were ordered to put on coats, hats and their boots. They were handcuffed and forced outside and into the back of Juan's car where the seat belts were strung through their handcuffs behind their backs. They were so tightly bound that they could barely move. The two kidnappers climbed in front and they took off down the driveway and down Thunder Lake Road, out to the highway.

"I gotta ask, just out of curiosity, where is the rest of the family?"

"They're probably all in the safe room in the basement," Mike says.

"Who are you and what do you want from us?" Audrey asks, "Are you FBI?"

"Oh no, not hardly, we are the ghosts of Christmas past," Juan says, "And you're going to talk to us about a shipment of drugs that went missing a year ago."

"We don't know anything about your drug shipment," Mike says.

"Oh, but we think you do and when we get where we're going, you're going to tell us all about it."

They drove along in silence then. They went south on Highway 6 until they came to a road called Washburn Lake Road. They turned and headed west, totally unaware that they were followed. That road wasn't plowed at all, so it was very slow going, sometimes they got stuck for a bit in the larger drifts.

* * * * * *

When Carlotta and the children, except Madeline were safe and secure in the panic room, Carlotta turned on one of the security camera screens. The system used infrared technology. One screen showed the kidnappers forcing Mike, Audrey and Madeline in the downstairs hall to put on their coats, hats and boots and depart out the door. Carlotta switched on another screen which showed them all getting into a car and heading down the driveway.

"Mom, I've got to go after them," Juanita exclaimed, "they've got Madeline and Grandma and Grandpa."

"But what can you do to stop them?"

"I have an idea, Mom. You call the police, from that phone over there. Remember, Grandpa said it's a special Satellite phone, in case the security system can't call out because the power's been cut off. I'm going to go after them on one of the snowmobiles. I can go faster than they can in deep snow."

With that Juanita grabbed a flashlight and ran to the door, opened it and was gone. As Carlotta picked the phone to call the police, they watched Juanita on the monitors; run up the stairs to the bedroom and got dressed, using the flashlight. The alarm was still blaring as she ran down the stairs and down the hall towards the garage. She stopped at the closet to put on her snowmobile suit, boots and helmet. She pulled something else out of the closet. They couldn't see what; the image was so poor with the infrared. She reached up on the shelf and took a small something and put it in her pocket. Another screen showed her in the garage. She opened the door, started up one of the snowmobiles and left, down the driveway and out into the howling blizzard.

Out on thunder Lake Road the visibility wasn't too bad, the thick stand of pine trees sheltered the road from the wind. But when she got out onto the highway, there was no stopping the wind and she felt the fill blunt of the blizzard. Thankfully the snowplow that had gone through earlier left a ridge of snow to guide her. She headed south on Highway 6, but had no idea how far ahead of her the kidnappers, her sister and her Grandma and Grandpa were. "What if they turned off somewhere?" she thought as she struggled to see through her snow covered goggles. She kept looking at the ridges of plowed snow, trying to see if they had turned off somewhere. She could only barely see the faint tracks left by their car.

After she had gone for what seemed like forever through the tunnel that her headlights created in the blackness and whiteout of the blizzard. Suddenly she realized that she wasn't seeing the tracks anymore. "Oh, no," she thought, "they've turned off somewhere behind me." She turned the snowmobile around and carefully watched for the spot where they turned off the main highway finally she spotted the turnoff, about a half mile back. She too, turned west and followed the now deeper tracks in the snow, because this road had not been plowed at all.

As she headed down the Washburn Lake Road, the snow seemed to be letting up slightly, but not the wind. The road wound its way around several small lakes and potholes at first, but then straightened out and headed straight west out of the heavily wooded state forest area and out into open farmland. Juanita wondered how far ahead of her they were. And, furthermore, where were they headed? After a few more miles, as she came up over the crest of a hill; there in the distance she could make out the faint red glow of tail lights. She immediately switched off her headlights so they wouldn't see someone following them. She struggled along in the dark. As long as she could see the red of the tail lights, they could guide her. The road was very straight ahead.

"Maybe." she thought, "She could close the gap between them."

They were about a mile and a half ahead of her, moving very slowly, struggling in the deep snow drifts. After some time, the snow stopped entirely. The moon began to shine through gaps in the clouds. The wind, however did not abate and kept drifting the new fallen snow across the open farmland. This limited her visibility and she had to slow down again. After several more miles, Juanita saw the tail lights brighten as the car braked and turned off the road.

* * * * * *

"What is this place?" Vasquez asked Juan.

"It's an abandoned farm. I discovered it last summer. It's very secluded. That grove of pine trees hides it from the road. I thought it would be the perfect place to conduct our little interrogations."

It was easier going up the long driveway. The wind was sweeping across the farm fields and blowing the snow off of the driveway.

There was no farmhouse. It had long ago either been torn down, moved, or rotted away after the farm family sold out. They were probably too old to farm anymore and moved into town and the kids all moved to the city to pursue a better life. All that was left was the barn and a silo. Juan pulled the car up to the barn door. He got out and opened the door while Vasquez unfastened the seatbelts of their passengers. Mike, Audrey and Madeline were forced into the old barn, while outside the blizzard wind was rattling the windows and piling up huge snow drifts around the ancient barn. The temperature was rapidly dropping into the minus below zero numbers. The old barn smelled like rotting ,musty hay and wood. The manure smell had long ago dissipated as the manure composted into black dirt.

The prisoners were taken by flashlight to a cow pen in the back of the barn; where there were several bales of the rotting hay sitting along the side of the pen. They were seated on the hay bales and tied up to the side of the pen. At this point, the three prisoners were pretty certain that they would not be leaving the barn alive.

Vasquez went back out to the car and came back with a couple of items. Juan said to the three prisoners, “Now we will talk.”

Vasquez lit the lantern he brought in from the trunk of the car and sat it on a hay bale in the middle of the pen. Vasquez set down the other objects he brought with him, a small propane torch and a branding iron. Juan Carlos began his interrogation as he approached Madeline.

"We'll start with you, my little pretty one. What can you tell me about that planeload of drugs that your father flew into the U.S. last year at Christmas?"

"I don't know anything about any drugs. My father was a pilot and flew all kinds of stuff all around Mexico. but he never flew any drugs into the U.S."

"Lying little bitch," He screamed at her as his temper began to rise and he punched her in the face and blood began to trickle down from her broken nose.

"Leave her alone," Audrey yelled at him, "Can't you tell she doesn't know anything about your drugs."

Juan stepped over to Audrey and back-handed her across her face, and her nose began to bleed as well

"You got something to say, bitch," He yelled at her, "Well here's a little something to get you started talking."

He grabbed the lantern from the bale of hay and took one of her hands and held it on top of the scorching hot lantern. Audrey screamed in pain as her hand blistered from the heat.

Mike yelled at Juan, "You cowardice bastard, that all you can do is torture and beat up innocent young girls and women?"

"Well, well then, you want your turn to talk. Here's what we want to know. Xavier Mendoza's plane carrying a load of drugs went down near Alamo Lake in Arizona last Christmas. That's what the DEA report said. We think you know exactly where that plane is. We also think you removed some or all of the drugs from the plane and may have sold them in Las Vegas. The cartel wants their drugs and the money back."

"I'm telling you, we don't know anything about your plane load of drugs at this Lake Alamo in Arizona. We've never ever been to this Lake Alamo."

"Here's the thing, Mister Felder," as he pushed his face hard into Mike's face, "We think you do, and soon you're going to tell us all about it. Vasquez, heat up your branding iron."

Vasquez brought out his branding iron and propane torch. The branding iron had the cartel emblem on it. He began heating up the iron until it was red hot. He ripped open Mike's coat and shirt. As he placed the red hot iron on mike's chest, the air became filled with the smell of burning flesh. Mike immediately began screaming and jumping around, a few seconds later his body stiffened and his eyes rolled back as he passed out. Vasquez then removed the branding iron.

* * * * * *

Juanita carefully and quietly pulled her snowmobile in behind the grove of pine trees, just out of sight of the barn. She shut it down and grabbed the case and quietly ran toward the barn as she heard screams even over the howling wind. She very quietly opened the barn door just a crack and peered inside. She could see the circle of the lantern light at the far end of the barn. She squeezed herself through the door very cautiously and quietly closed the door behind her and crept down the aisle way toward the back of the barn, closer to the light. She entered a cow pen just across the aisle, but outside the circle of lantern light. She took up a position behind the cow pen's manger and set the gun case down on a bale of hay and very silently slid the case latches open and took out the twelve gauge shotgun.

She thanked God that just two days ago, Grandpa Mike had taken her and her brother Juan down the trail on their snowmobiles to a very remote, secluded place where they set up the skeet thrower. Mike would load a clay pigeon into the arm of the thrower and pull the spring loaded arm back and lock it into place. She and Juan took turns standing a ways off with the shotgun at the ready. They would yell ‘pull’ when they were set. Grandpa would pull a cord releasing the arm, and the clay pigeon would go flying out in a high arc across in front of them at some distance. It took quite a few clay pigeons before they started hitting them. Soon though they became quite good at hitting the clays.

Juanita carefully took the shotgun shells out of her pocket and very quietly loaded four of them into the chamber and tube of the shotgun. She rested the gun on the top of the manger and peered across the aisle into the other cow pen.

* * * * * *

In the other cow pen, Audrey and Madeline sat there in complete shock at what had just happened to Mike. They all just waited. Five minutes, then ten went by. Finally Mike slowly regained consciousness. He painfully moaned as he open his eyes.

“Well, now,” Juan said , “Are you ready to tell me where that drug plane is at Alamo Lake, and the money you got from selling some of the drugs in Vegas?”

Mike couldn’t answer yet, he was still semiconscious. He slurred his words as he tried to say, "I don't know about a plane at Alamo Lake."

"I'll give you another minute to think about that. Vasquez is ready to fire up the iron again."

"Enough, enough, "Audrey shouted, but before she could utter the words, "We'll tell you everything," Juan stepped over and yelled at her, "Shut the hell up, bitch, nobody asked you," and backhanded her in the face, blooding her lip and knocking out several teeth. He went back over to Madeline.

"So, you little bitch, where did your papa tell you he landed his plane?"

"I never saw my father again after that Christmas."

"You're a lying little bitch. I'm getting pretty angry here, and you're going to pay a price if you don't start talking."

With that he went up to Madeline and tore her coat off and ripped down her pants.

"Okay you little whore, Juanita, do you want me to have to rape you just like the last two times?"

"I'm not Juanita," Madeline shouted back at him, "I'm Madeline."

With that Juanita picked up the shotgun and stepped out of the shadows and into the cow pen. Juan Carlos heard her enter and turned toward her, grabbing his gun as he turned.

She aimed the shotgun at him but, just as he was about to fire his gun at her, he stepped forward and tripped over the bale of hay. His shot went wild, up into the ceiling. As he tried to regain his balance she fired her shotgun, aiming for his head, but missed as he fell forward. Some of the pellets however, went through his neck, severing his spine at C-4. He dropped to the floor like a sack of rocks, although not dead, paralyzed for the rest of his short life.

The sound of the shotgun in the confined space of the cow pen shocked and deafened everyone else. When Vasquez recovered, he picked up his gun from the bale of hay and pointed it at Mike, still sprawled out on his bale of hay and turned and yelled at Juanita, "Drop your shotgun, you bitch, or your Grandpa here is a dead man."

Juanita aimed and pulled her trigger again and hit him in his right shoulder and his gun went flying. He dropped back onto a bale of hay like a rock, screaming and rolling around and grabbing at his shoulder. However, two shots could be heard, a split second apart. As Vasquez was hit, his finger was on the trigger and the impact of the shotgun caused the gun to fire. The round hit Mike in the upper chest. Lucky for him, he was lying flat out on his back on the bale of hay. The bullet entered just above his left lung, and because of the angle, it traveled upwards under his collar bone, shattering his shoulder that he just recently had replaced.

Juanita dropped the shotgun onto a hay bale and ran to her sister and untied her, then dug into Juan Carlos's pocket and got the keys and unlocked all their handcuffs. Madeline pulled up her pants and closed up her jacket best she could.

Audrey checked Mike's wound as he passed out again. "Hurry", she told the girls, "he's wounded pretty bad. We've got to get him to a hospital."

She tore off a large piece of his shirt and made a pressure bandage for the wound. She zipped up his coat tightly around his upper chest and shoulder to hold his shoulder in place. Together the three of them carefully carried him out to the car and placed him in the back seat. Juanita ran back into the barn to get the car keys out of Juan Carlos's pocket. Audrey and Madeline followed. The two cartel thugs were still laying there.

Juanita said, "Come on, let's just go. Let them just bleed out and die. It would serve them right after what they did to my family and me."

"No Juanita," Audrey said, "We can't just leave them here to die. We have to do what we can to save their lives. They are still human, after all. They will have to answer to God for their many crimes against other humans. And they will have to face the U.S. justice system for their crimes against the USA."

Audrey and the girls got busy and first bandaged Vasquez's shoulder.

"About all we can do for him is stop the bleeding," Audrey said, "He'll probably lose his arm."

They did the same for Juan Carlos. They stopped the bleeding in his neck wound. Luckily for him, no arteries were severed. They took the ropes that had tied them up to the cow pen wall and tied up the two cartel thugs securely.

"Wait, wait," Vasquez whined, "You can't just leave us here. We'll freeze to death."

"Well, now, wouldn't that be just too bad," Juanita said, "After what you and your partner just did, it would be a fitting ending for you both."

But, before they left, the three girls took apart several of the hay bales and covered the two evil thugs with the hay to keep them from freezing to death. They told them that they would send help and law enforcement.

The girls closed the barn door and all got in the front seat of Juan Carlos's car. Audrey drove as fast as she could through the drifting snow covered road and out to Highway 6 and south toward the town of Aitkin. They got to the Aitkin

County Hospital ER in about forty five minutes. There was a surgeon just wrapping up a surgery from a traffic accident. Mike was rushed into surgery. The surgery took a long time. There was a lot of damage to Mike's collar bone and shoulder requiring a lot of screws and pins. A skin graft was placed over his branding burn.

While they waited Juanita called Carlotta at the lake cabin. She reported that she couldn't get through to the sheriff, so they waited for about an hour to come out of the safe room and then she figured out how to turn the electricity back on. The children all went back to bed, but she stayed up waiting to hear that everyone was okay.

Audrey had to fill out the paperwork while they waited, along with a police report because it was a gunshot injury. She wrote it up as a break in and the assailant ran off into the blizzard, which wasn't too far from the truth. She had to protect the Mendoza children. But she then knew that they had to go back and clean up that crime scene before anyone came across it. The surgeon reported to her after the surgery, that while he repaired most of the damage from the bullet, Mike would need another surgery to try and remove a bone chip that was lodged dangerously close to his spine. So he would have to remain lying down and immobile for up to a week before they could do that surgery.

While Mike was in the recovery room, Audrey explained to Juanita and Madeline that they needed to return to that barn and clean it up. It contained all of their fingerprints and DNA. That would be a problem for the girls because they were not citizens and could be deported back to Mexico for being involved in a crime.

The three girls returned to the crime scene. The temperature was now about minus twenty degrees below zero. As they opened up the barn door they could hear a faint moan. Juan Carlos was apparently still alive. Lucky for them both, the cold had slowed down the bleeding from their wounds. Juan Carlos couldn't yell or talk of course because his whole body was paralyzed. Vasquez begged them to get him to someplace warm.

"I think I'm freezing to death here,"

The girls first dragged Vasquez out to the car and used one of the handcuffs to handcuff him to the inside door handle. Next they dragged Juan Carlos's barely alive body out to the car. They didn't need to restrain him, because he was completely paralyzed. No more would these two terrorize, torture and murder innocent victims. They removed the propane torch, branding iron, ropes, handcuffs and the lantern from the barn and loaded them back into the car trunk of the car. They closed the barn doors and latched them. The shotgun they took with them. It was registered to Mike. Juanita and Madeline got on the snowmobile and headed back to the cabin. The blizzard winds had calmed down and the morning sky was showing a faint pinkish line just above the horizon as Audrey returned to the Aitkin hospital where Mike was just coming too. She turned the two cartel thugs in to the ER and called the sheriff and the FBI to finish dealing with them. When Mike was fully conscious she explained to him what she and the girls had done.

"Good job, Honey. Pray to God that we never hear from that Medellin cartel. and it's agents again. Those two and that cartel are the devil's disciples."

THE END

EPILOGUE

Mike and Audrey had to spend many hours with the FBI, the DEA, and ICIS explaining what had happened. Juan Carlos died from his neck wound shortly after serving several years of his life sentence. Vasquez is still serving multiple life sentences somewhere in a federal prison.

After Mike's second surgery and his release from the hospital, the family packed up and left their cabin and returned to the city. The children all returned to school. Their lives returned to normal.

They did not, however, ever return to their lake house again. The next spring, Mike and Audrey decided to sell the place. In spite of all the good memories created there, the horrors of that Christmas could not be erased.

As the years went by, the Mendoza and Ramirez children all finished school and became citizens and went on to college. Like the countless millions of immigrants before them that make up this great country, they became productive citizens and had families of their own.

Gradually the memories of those two horrific Christmases faded into the distant past.

The two snowbirds never again returned to Arizona, although they thought about it a lot and talked about that last fateful snowbird trip.

They have this warning to all the snowbirds who decide to fly away for the winter, to Lake Havasu City, Arizona: - - - -

Don't go exploring up the Bill Williams River, and if you do, do not find a small creek flowing out of a deep dark canyon.

Do not follow this creek up into that dark canyon. Turn around and run.

But if you do follow that creek into that dark canyon, do not stop and look at the wreckage of those two airplanes. Run like the devil from it.

But if you do look at the wreckage, do not look up; high above the canyon, about fifty feet up the sheer rock cliff, there on a ledge with a rocky overhang, you would see a large dark object wedged into the rocks.

Run like the devil from this place. This is your last warning, - - - - - Do not even think about climbing that cliff to have a closer look. Please, please, please believe me. You will be sucked into a nightmare trip of unbelievable horror.

Turn around and run like the devil. This is a portal to the underworld. a gateway into hell. This place is haunted by the lost souls of that plane crash. The devil himself lives here in the form of the ghosts of Juan Carlos and his murdering, torturing partner Vasquez and the damned souls of the ruthless Medellin Cartel rulers. This is the devils playground. Run like the devil!!!

ACKNOWLEDGEMENTS

Thanks to my lovely wife Barbara, for the love and support she gives me, in this and all my writing adventures. Barbara is my quintessential chief editor.

Thanks to Daughter-In-Law, Carla Fellerer, Artist and Illustrator, for her work on the cover.

Thanks for the inspiration of all the snowbirds who venture forth every winter to bask under the blue skies and eternal sunshine of Arizona. Most especially Sue and George who always make us feel welcome to the warm place that they now call home.

To all of our children, grandchildren and the great grandchildren all of whom we always miss appreciably while we are off on our adventurous sojourns into the deserts of the southwest.

* * * * * * * * * *

Go to WWW.otterfallspublishing.com to see more background about these new books in the Otter Falls series:

PIONEERS ON THE OTTERTAIL
MYSTERY ON THE OTTERTAIL
ADVENTURES ON THE OTTERTAIL
RETURN TO OTTER FALLS

Take a look at the new releases by;
ROBB FELDER

LAST FLIGHT OF THE SNOWBIRDS
THE COLD COLD WAR

AND;
DEATH OF A BREWERY
To be available late summer, 2019

ROBB FELDER Is a Vietnam Veteran. He attended the University of Alaska and the University of Minnesota. He is the author of THE OTTER FALLS SERIES. a trilogy of historical novels. Robb is retired from a successful career as a computer applications software designer. He and his wife Barbara live in a suburb of the Twin Cities of Minnesota.

www.ingramcontent.com/pod-product-compliance
Lightning Source LLC
Chambersburg PA
CBHW060946120726
47910CB00002B/515

* 9 7 8 1 0 8 7 8 5 6 8 8 9 *